THE ROGANS

They dwelt in darkness, shunning all light, and flew the night skies, red eyes gleaming, endlessly seeking prey to sate their lust for blood. But now the Rogans had done the unforgivable—they'd killed a member of the Space Exploratory Forces—and it was up to Morgan Farraday, agent extraordinaire, to see that it didn't happen again. But the key to this mysterious and hideous murder lay in the forbidden domain of the Rogans' city—and would the price of entry for Morgan be her own life's blood?

Seven Worlds

Mary Caraker

A SIGNET BOOK

NEW AMERICAN LIBRARY

NAL BOOKS ARE AVAILABLE AT QUANTITY DISCOUNTS WHEN
USED TO PROMOTE PRODUCTS OR SERVICES. FOR INFORMATION
PLEASE WRITE TO PREMIUM MARKETING DIVISION, NEW AMERI-
CAN LIBRARY, 1633 BROADWAY, NEW YORK, NEW YORK 10019.

Acknowledgments

"A Thrrup for Teacher," copyright © 1984 by Davis Publications, Inc.
"The Vampires Who Loved Beowulf," copyright © 1982 by Davis
    Publications, Inc.
These stories originally appeared in *Analog Science Fiction/
Science Fact Magazine.*

SIGNET TRADEMARK REG. U.S. PAT. OFF. AND FOREIGN COUNTRIES
REGISTERED TRADEMARK—MARCA REGISTRADA
HECHO EN CHICAGO, U.S.A.

SIGNET, SIGNET CLASSIC, MENTOR, ONYX, PLUME, MERIDIAN AND
NAL BOOKS are published by New American Library,
1633 Broadway, New York, New York 10019

First Printing, September, 1986

1 2 3 4 5 6 7 8 9

PRINTED IN THE UNITED STATES OF AMERICA

To my mother,
Hilma Lumijarvi

Prologue

The young woman wore the trim green dress uniform of the Space Corps. Her fresh complexion and slender figure belied the rows of service bars on her shoulders, but there was something about her steady gaze and the firm set of her mouth that confirmed the evidence of the emblems.

"Morgan Farraday?" The man behind the desk stood up.

Morgan extended her hand. His was soft, she noted, and his grasp lacked tone. Years spent at a keyboard and screen, she guessed. Probably in his mid-thirties, with no field experience.

How typical of SEF bureaucracy, she thought, to give a desk officer the power to decide if she was still fit for the outer reaches. An Academy management type who probably hadn't been off Central Station in his entire career.

There was no call for bitterness, though, she cautioned herself. This man was her final hurdle. She squared her shoulders and gave him a bright smile.

"Leo Billingsgate," the man said, motioning her to a chair. He sat, too, and shuffled the thick sheaf of printouts on his desk top. "I must admit I'm surprised at this request. At your age, to volunteer for another teaching assignment. . ."

"My chronological age has nothing to do with

it," Morgan said. "According to the 'special cir-
cumstances' clause, I'm still eligible if I can
pass the physicals. The results of my latest ones
must be in there." She indicated the stack of
papers.

He nodded. "Yes, I've seen them, and they're. . .
remarkable. I'm not worried about that aspect.
What concerns me is your psychological profile.
I'd like to hear more about your past assignments. How they affected you, and how you feel
about them now."

"You have all the reports."

"I do, but I'd rather hear it in your own words,
if you don't mind. Sometimes there are
. . . things a written review doesn't catch. We
wouldn't want to send you out if there's any
chance of a dysfunction."

Morgan groaned to herself. He was the sort
who performed his duties exactingly. This would
be no perfunctory interview, and she might as
well get on with it. "Okay," she said. "What do
you want to know?"

"Everything. Just relax and relive it all." He
leaned back in his chair and steepled his fingers. "Now, you were first posted to Parth, right?
Do you remember your early days there?"

Parth. Yes, she remembered it well. . . .

I. A *Thrrup* for Teacher

It appeared on Morgan's desk the second day of school: a vile-smelling gelatinous gray mound the size of a softball; slimy—like everything, it seemed to her, on this swamp of a planet—and vibrating obscenely. She conquered her shudder (*tact, tact*, the indoctrination tapes had stressed, *don't display aversion, whatever you may find strange*), managed a faint smile, and peered closer. The movement, she saw, was caused by a mass of wriggling white maggots.

Tact be damned! Morgan choked and ran for the door. Gulps of cool air and a facewash in the misty rain finally settled her rebellious stomach, but her nerves remained raw. Friendly and docile, were they, these children of Parth? Obedient and eager to please? So she'd been promised, for her first assignment, but it appeared she'd been duped. Two days into the job and already she'd been patted and poked by slimy scaled hands, her hair had been pulled almost out by the roots, her clothing had been ripped, and she'd given up trying to keep them in their seats. And now they had succeeded in making her lose control completely.

She wouldn't allow them the satisfaction, though, of knowing how undone she was. Morgan wiped her face and straightened her shoulders. She had dressed for combat today, in sturdy khaki that couldn't be torn and her hair was neatly secured in a braid. If only she felt as tough and competent as she looked, she thought. But she'd brave it out—she had to, for what threatened to be a make-or-break year.

She had suspected something fishy when she had been rushed with such haste to Parth as soon as she had completed her language training. Then it had been straight to the school, with no proper indoctrination; only the tapes and the scant information supplied by her supervisor, Captain Kraskolin, when he had settled her in. The teacher before her had left unexpectedly—"flew the coop," she had heard at the spaceport—and the captain had confirmed it.

"The kind of irresponsible behavior that gives the Corps a bad name," he had said, eyeing her uneasily as if searching for symptoms of similar flightiness.

She had assured him of her intention to fulfill her contract, and he had relaxed. Space Exploratory Forces needed their toehold on Parth for strategic reasons, he had explained, and the Parthians had to be kept happy. The Space Corps, teaching arm of SEF, established native schools only when they were requested, and after years of insularity from their bizarre but well-paying guests the Parthians suddenly *wanted* their children to learn Terran. "So they can monitor us in the future," Kras had said pointedly.

"Don't they trust us?" Morgan had asked

"Would you?" His mouth had twisted into a wry smile. "They may be uncivilized by our standards, but they're no dummies. SEF has really put the Corps on the spot. If we don't satisfy the Parthian Council of Elders—pfft! Out we all go, schools and base and maybe even the port."

"So how many schools do we have here now?"

"Half a dozen, including this one. But so far"
—running a hand through his shock of damp
curls—"we haven't had any breakthrough. The
other teachers are all experienced, and God
knows they're trying. That's why we particularly wanted a young, fresh teacher here. Your
predecessor, Mr. Tiptin—well, the less said about
him the better. He's the reason I've instituted a
three-week trial period."

"To check up on me?" She hadn't been able to
disguise her disappointment; she had thought
herself through with probation. Her second
thought had been no more comforting. "Or to
see if I'm still here?"

He had smiled. "To offer you what help I can.
I'm new to Parth myself, but anything I can
do. . ."

It had been Morgan's turn to thaw. The captain was tall and lean and neatly bearded, with
the warmest brown eyes she had seen under any
sun. He had spent a whole day getting her
squared away, providing her with the tapes, with
friendly advice and a great deal of encourage-
ment.

But still she had been unprepared. For unhu-
man squeaks and grasping hands and worm rid-
den lumps.

The class was quiet when she reentered the
hut, and the nasty object was gone. There would
be no point in trying to find the culprit, she
decided. Far from being able to recognize guilt,
she couldn't even distinguish yet between the
faces.

Twenty expressionless ciphers stared up at
her. Twenty identical pairs of protruding, heavy-
lidded eyes, twenty flat slitted noses and chin-
less jaws. Gray scaly skin and mustard-colored
hair that grew like a fungus down their necks
and backs and even between their fingers and

toes. They smelled of fungus, too—a musty odor,
like a decaying swamp, that pervaded the room.

Morgan straightened again and stared back
with what she hoped was dignity. Yesterday she
had started out informally, with disastrous results. "Good morning," she said in careful
Parthian. "I am happy to see you all again. Let
us proceed with the lesson."

A small boy in the first row slid down in his
seat and rested his feet on the desk top, a position in which his genitals, beneath the short
fringed skirt, were distressingly visible to Morgan. Several others adopted similar positions or
slid out completely to squat on the floor. The
nose and head picking began.

Morgan summoned up the tape: *Remember,
your sole function is to teach them Terran. Forget
about manners and mores. They have requested
language teachers, so stick to that or you may do
the Corps irreparable harm.*

Okay, she would ignore the manners. Probably to them picking and feeling were perfectly
acceptable behavior for kids. She got out the
picture cards. "Mother," she said, holding up
the sketch of a Parthian woman with children.
"Ranillin," she repeated in Parthian, to be sure
they made the connection.

The children struggled with the sounds. Gig-
gles and touchy-feely interrupted the lesson, but
Morgan stubbornly continued to drill them. She
concentrated on smaller groups, whenever she
could get their attention, but to little avail. By
the end of the hour the children still could not
say, recognizably, a single Terran word. Morgan
was exhausted and the room was a chaos of
disarranged desks and squirming small bodies.

She didn't understand it. Donald Tiptin had
been teaching them phonics, according to his
notes. The children should have learned at least
the basic sounds. 'How many of you were in

school before, with Mr. Tiptin?" she asked in Parthian.

"Tlip-tlin!" came a chorus of shouts and screaming laughter. "Tlip-tlin!" The children pounded on the desks and collapsed hysterically in the aisles.

That was one name she'd never mention again, Morgan vowed. She consulted her records and saw that most of her students had been in Tiptin's class. They must have learned something besides a garbled version of his name.

But when she tried the phonics she got no response. It was time for recess, she decided, and herded the children outside. She straightened the furniture and swept up the mud they had tracked in, then set out pencils and paper for a writing lesson.

Morgan liked a tidy classroom. Teaching had appealed to her as an orderly profession where she could do useful work in a pleasant, structured setting. But the only openings had turned out to be in the Space Corps, and this particular setting was about as unstructured as she could imagine. And as for the work—if the first two days were any indication, she would have only failure to show when Captain Kraskolin came by for his inspection.

She sighed, and distributed crayons in brightly decorated cans. She tacked up model letters on a display board, refusing to think of yesterday and the disgusting uses to which her precious supplies had been put.

She watched the children from the doorway of her stilted hut as they played happily in the rain—laughing piebald figures scampering lightly over the soggy field into which, earlier that morning out for her exercise, she had squished awkwardly. Parth was a rain planet, a water planet, its marshes and spreading dark forests nourished by the steady precipitation—torrential in winter and now, in the summer months, an almost constant light drizzle which the children seemed not to notice.

At the edge of the clearing they raced around and beneath the fernlike trees, swinging on the ropy lichen that bearded the twining purple fronds. From a distance they looked like the children she had imagined and expected; like the innocent creatures she had been prepared to love.

She had listened, unconvinced, to the Corps lectures on culture shock. Kids were the same everywhere, she had told herself, finding something cute in all the slides, even the baby Rogans with their fangs and claws. The Parthians had actually seemed among the most "human" of the alien sapients. But that had been from a safe distance. She hadn't seen the fungus or the scales or smelled that rank odor of decay.

Or felt their prying, inquisitive fingers, she thought later. She had summoned them inside and forgotten to station herself safely behind the barricade of her desk. They rushed upon her, chirping and trilling and clicking in excited talk punctuated by the continual, ceaseless poking and pressing. A dozen hands grabbed hers.

"Did you see me swing? I was higher than Gvran."

"Yes, but you fell. Teacher, my arms are stronger. Feel."

"When can we eat? Feel my stomach empty."

"Why does your skin feel dry and smooth? Where is your hair behind?"

A cold raspy hand reached up her back beneath her shirt. The odor was suffocating. "Cut it out! Get back!" she shouted in Terran, then in Parthian. She pushed away the hands.

Morgan didn't stop shaking until they were all safely seated in orderly rows. Then she steadied herself by concentrating on the lesson. She carefully patterned for them the letter A.

Papers tore as the small hands gripped their pencils awkwardly and pressed too hard. Again she was surprised at how little they knew—she would have to teach them to hold a pencil. Fighting against her aversion, she opened the moss-furred fingers and guided the scaly hands in their first motions.

The children quickly mastered the pencils, but the letters defeated them. They screwed up their faces into frightening grimaces while filling their papers with squiggles. And before she could gather the papers, remembering yesterday's fiasco, they ended up torn and crumpled and chewed into gummy wads.

It wasn't quite time for lunch break, but she excused them early. She had to air out the hut before she herself could think of eating.

In her cubbyhole of a studio behind the classroom she ate a cold meal straight from the packets. The tapes again echoed: *A big plus, if you can tolerate the native diet.* Sure I can, she had thought, as long as it's safe. But the grubs, the molds, the stringy waterweeds?

The children were back much too soon, smelling even stronger of whatever unlikely concoction they'd had for lunch. Morgan had moved the desks aside and put out toys on the floor for the afternoon session. She couldn't push her class too hard, she had decided, or she might lose them all. In the morning there had already been two fewer than yesterday, and now when she counted again there were only eighteen.

What stories had they told their parents? she wondered. Maybe she wouldn't even have a class in three weeks. Tiptin, at least, had held onto his students.

The children bent busily over puzzles and pegboards, adeptly fitting shapes into holes and

linking slotted blocks into elaborate structures.
Morgan squatted beside a spindly-legged girl
who was playing with an abacus and guided the
child's hand to arrange the beads into groups of
two, then four. The Parthian understood immediately and correctly worked further additions.

Maybe it was a handle to teach them language! Hopeful for the first time, Morgan fetched
a small slate (no more wasting paper, she had
decided) and chalked in the number two. "Two,
two," she repeated, signaling the child to repeat.

"Thrrk," the small girl trilled and clicked in
Parthian. She demolished the chalk and blew
dust in Morgan's face, then turned back to the
abacus.

Morgan walked away, her face burning. She
would have shaken a Terran child and set him
in a corner. Sent home a note. But here—she
didn't even know if the girl had meant to be
rude. No one else paid much attention to the
incident; their fingers were as busy, their faces
as unreadable as ever.

The remainder of the week was just as bad.
Morgan made no progress teaching either spoken language or letters. She had to conclude
that the children were simply being stubborn—
there was no reason why they couldn't learn
Terran. Granted, it was vastly different from
Parthian, but Morgan had mastered the tongue-
trills and rolls and guttural clicks, and there
was no physical barrier to the children's pro-
nouncing Terran vowels and consonants.

But they wouldn't try, just as they refused to
copy the alphabet. Afternoon play was the only
activity that interested them at all, and the only
reason, she suspected, why they continued to
come.

Certainly not because of her. She had pushed
them away too often, and they no longer crowded

around her, reached prying fingers, or asked her to "feel my stomach." As a teacher, a friend, or even a curiosity, she was totally ignored. She should have been relieved, hating as she did their touch; but instead, perversely, she felt rejected, which added to her growing sense of defeat.

She had been warned about the loneliness, but it got to her more than she had expected. She had only one human visitor the entire week. Dawes the trader arrived on an afternoon after school—fat-bellied, red-eyed space flotsam whom she would ordinarily have despised. She welcomed him like a brother.

He came crashing through the forest in a landsled, gouging huge muddy tracks across the field and up to her door. After he unloaded a plexicrate of supplies he sprawled at her desk.

"So why've they stuck a doll like you out here in the boonies? That gimp that was here before, sure, but you—what a waste! Claws of a Rogan, there's nothing out here but *kiri*-trees and swamp. And shit-furred monkey-men!"

He laughed uproariously at his idea of a joke, and Morgan smiled thinly. Traders were godsends in isolated areas, but she wished he could have been someone more . . . personable.

"But what're you doing out here?" he repeated. "Bothrup's not much of a burg, but at least it's got streets and houses and a coupla bars. And humans. Why can't you teach over there?"

"This is where the children are, not in the towns," she explained patiently. "The Corps has a half-dozen teachers on Parth, and they're all in rural areas like this. The Parthians built their schools where *they* wanted them."

"Tough for you, eh, chickie?" He leered, a parody of a smile. "I've seen some of the other warhorses the Corps sent, and I wouldn't feel sorry for *them*. But you—it's a damn waste of talent."

"So how long have you been out here?" she asked, to get his attention away from her. "Do you eventually get used to the rain?"

He snorted. "In a Rogan's eye! I've been here five years, and I'd give up five more to get off. But every time I try to save up the credits ..." He swigged from an imaginary bottle and winked. "Hell, it's the only thing that keeps me going on this waterlogged pisspot of a planet."

She managed another strained smile. Dawes could be a useful source of information. "It's wet, I'll grant you that," she said. "Tell me: how do you get along with the natives?"

"By holding my nose!" He roared again, slapping his oilskin-covered thigh. "Took me two years just to savvy the lingo, and that's always been easy for me. But I couldn't get close enough to talk to them—know what I mean?" He squinted around the small closed classroom, and sniffed. "Sure you do—I can still smell it in here. It's what they eat, I think—you seen their food?"

"Some of it." She remembered the wormy lump that had been her first present, and described it. "Was that supposed to scare me, or should I have thanked someone?"

He grinned. "Lady, you got the prize. I mean, that's a *thrrup*—a sort of a well-aged mushroom. It's like an ice cream cone to them kids—best thing they could give you. You must sure rate with them."

Not anymore, she thought. She suddenly felt cross and depressed, and wished he would leave. She served the obligatory cup of coffee and listened to his further fulminations against the planet and its monkey-men and the general way life had treated him.

"You must get pretty lonely out here, eh?" He was becoming personal again.

"No, I don't," she said firmly.

He ignored her rebuff. "Now, I don't hafta rush right off. I could spend the night—even stay a coupla days. How'd that suit ya?" He grabbed her chin and pulled her face toward him. The hairs in his nose were stiff and black.

She twisted free. She wasn't really frightened— one bad report from her and he would lose his license, and he knew it. "Watch it," she warned. "I said no!" If he persisted, or got rough, she had her finger-needle. She ran her thumb lightly over the release.

He backed off. "Now don't get uppity. I only meant, if you felt like it. Me, I can get it any time in Bothrup."

"Never seen a Space Corps dame yet wasn't a block of ice," he mumbled, getting up.

To you, maybe. She said it to herself. To him she spoke civil goodbyes and gave a large new order; she couldn't afford to make an enemy.

She saw him off with relief. Dawes must know she was just a probationer, she thought; if she won her spurs and remained, he would never dare try anything again.

If she remained. At the moment it seemed a remote possibility. Morgan paced the *kiri*-floored room until she became claustrophobic, then pulled on boots and a slicker and climbed down the ladder to tramp the clearing.

The spongy mire discouraged her before she had made a complete circuit, and she headed for the trees and firmer ground. In the forest the carpet of humus made an easier footing, but the crawling vines and trailing rope-fingers fought her and dripped on her until she turned back in sodden defeat.

There was nowhere to go, anyway. Bothrup was a day's hike, with no trail. Parthian homesteads were scattered in the forest, but even if

she had wanted to visit, courtesy forbade her to
invade their privacy without an invitation.

And there would be none, she knew, unless
she somehow reversed whatever it was she was
doing wrong. The Parthians expected the schools
to succeed, and she didn't know how patient
they were. Somehow she had to get through to
those baffling children.

During the one-day break (a concession to Terran customs; the Parthians observed no week-
ends), Morgan reviewed her library of tapes and
slides for clues. The information was all familiar: *The Parthian children are allowed a great deal
of freedom.* That, she knew! *They are curious and
outgoing until puberty, when they become reticent
and fiercely protective of their privacy.*

Okay, they had to be reached early. But how?
She studied more material—their homes, their
economy, their social and tribal structures—but
none of it seemed pertinent to her problem. Donald Tiptin's ill-kept records were no help either.
"Continue with drills and seat-work *if you can*,"
he had written, before he had fled. Apparently
he had let the children do pretty much as they
pleased.

And she had inherited his mess. However, she
was grimly determined not to give up. Besides
her own pride, there was Captain Kraskolin,
who had been so kind and supportive that she
couldn't bear to confront him with her failure.

Kind, yes—but she admitted to herself that it
was more than that. Those eyes ... "I really
hope you'll change our luck," Kras had said.
She had probably read too much into his smile,
but living as she did in isolation she couldn't
help daydreaming.

Only two more weeks—to prove herself or have
the captain pack her out again, a financial loss
to the Corps and a burden to the Terran settle-

ment until the next Earthside rocket came. "God knows they're trying," he had said of the other teachers. He would probably think she wasn't. Another Tiptin, he would most likely consider her. Perhaps he would assign her to one of the other schools, an unwanted assistant.

The day stretched long, and Morgan sought refuge in housework. The Parthians had provided her with luxuries—like heat and running water—that must have seemed laughable to them. She scraped fungus from her shower and from the recesses of her storage bins. She washed her clothes and strung them to dry across the schoolroom, firing her stove to aid the process. She routed split-tailed crawlers from behind the corner beams, but gave up when she saw that they were inaccessibly established in the roof thatch. As long as they didn't come out. . .

She took down her wash and scrubbed her floor until the *kiri*-swirls gleamed. She polished the desks and arranged them in geometric precision. The room shone. It proclaimed order and industry, and she felt a proud sense of accomplishment.

Discipline. That was the key, she thought. *Control.* Concepts foreign to the Parthian children. She had been too soft, too timid, letting them dictate to her. Another Tiptin. The children *could* learn, if only they would stop their incessant play and focus their minds.

It was her answer. She had to teach them to concentrate, and that meant sitting still, much as they seemed to hate it. The desks would stay in their positions, the children would stay at the desks, and the hands would stay on the desktops. There would be no feely games during classtime, and it had nothing to do with mores— only with doing her job as a teacher.

*   *   *

It wasn't easy, but Morgan persevered in her role of stern-faced martinet. By lunch break the next day she had fifteen subdued little figures sitting bolt upright, hands on desks and eyes fixed reproachfully on hers.

At last she had their complete attention. She held up the familiar picture. "Mah-ther," she pronounced slowly for the hundredth time.

And received absolutely no response.

She made an inspiring little speech about industry and success and how they could all say the words if they would only listen to her and try.

The children wriggled uncomfortably, and the smallest ones swallowed hiccups that sounded suspiciously like sobs.

Morgan tried a few words, but received only hostile stares. She excused them for lunch.

It would take time, she told herself; at least she had made the first step. The tear-filled eyes of little Skrril troubled her, but she reminded herself that she was here to teach, not to win a popularity contest. And without distractions, Skrril and the others *would* begin to learn.

Unfortunately, Skrril did not return from lunch. Neither did two others. Morgan drilled the remaining twelve children in phonics, but even with such a small class she made no headway. In the writing lesson squiggles still covered the slates.

The next day only ten children appeared. Morgan was well into another one-sided oral lesson when three Parthian adults appeared in the doorway.

They filed in silently and flattened themselves against the rear wall. The children did not blink, and Morgan knew that she must follow suit—it was discourteous of the visitors to invade *her* space, and she would be even ruder to acknowledge them.

She pretended that they were not there and went on with her monologue that should have been a dialogue.

"Good morning." No answer.

"How are you?" Silence.

"Fine, thank you. My name is Mary—what is yours? My name is John, my name is ..." She rattled on without pausing for the missing responses, disconcerted by the silent watchers. They had to be really concerned, she knew, to appear unannounced the way they did.

Of course, the children had talked. Complained. The elders had to find out what was going on.

Parthian children are allowed a great deal of freedom. She had probably overstepped completely.

Morgan tried not to look at her visitors, but their image was stamped on her mind: three gaunt figures in leathery fringed skirts nearly to their ankles, motionless as statues but radiating disapproval; the eyes, shielded by the heavy lids, missing nothing.

Demoralized by the silent scrutiny, Morgan ran out of words. She began reading the dictionary until it dropped from her shaking hands. She felt like an idiot.

This was insane, she decided; why couldn't she simply find out what they wanted? She looked at the men directly and started toward the back of the room. "How may I help you?" she asked in Parthian.

The three visitors disappeared as quickly and silently as they had entered.

School was short that day. What did it matter, Morgan thought, when it was all so useless? Her authoritarian methods had only made the kids more unreachable, and now it appeared that the Parthians themselves would see to her dismissal even before Captain Kraskolin.

Two children lingered after the rest were

gone—Lurrp, the chalk-blowing mathematician, and Tillin, a sober little boy whose fingers had been particularly adept with the slotted blocks. Lurrp worked her hands nervously as she asked in Parthian trills: "Teacher, will we have play with the finger shapes tomorrow?"

Morgan had not brought out the toys all week, part of her new campaign. Her failed campaign.

Why not? she thought, and was about to answer when Tillin poked an inquisitive finger into the soft flesh of her backside.

She jumped and lashed out angrily, in Parthian: "Stop it! Haven't I told you to keep your hands away from me?" Tillin's face crumpled (when had she thought the Parthians expressionless?), and he retreated hastily—down the ladder and across the clearing before Morgan could undo her harshness. Lurrp gave her a sorrowful glance and glided out, too.

Morgan gave up all hope when only six children showed up the next day. One of them was Lurrp, but the thin girl looked so sad-mouthed that Morgan wondered why she had bothered to come. The lure of the abacus?

She might as well let them play, she decided, and spilled out the toys.

The children slid joyfully from the stiff chairs. Lurrp claimed the abacus and stroked it lovingly, crooning to herself. When she looked up to meet Morgan's gaze, she held out the toy.

The beads were arranged in groups of two. Lurrp strained, open-mouthed, to form a word.

Morgan knelt beside her, expecting nothing, her mind as woodenly blank as her automatic response. She enunciated slowly, with exaggerated lip movements, "Toooo."

Lurrp reached hesitant fingers to Morgan's mouth and felt the expulsion of air.

The touch was cold and the rank smell of

mossy fingers filled Morgan's nostrils. Her every instinct was to slap away the hand, but she could feel the eagerness, the *wanting* in Lurrp, and she did not move. Suddenly overcome by the futility of everything she had done, had tried to do, her defenses crumbled. She was tired of her stiff-backed pose, tired of keeping the children forever at a distance, tired of uselessly protesting.

She repeated the word, and while the fingers explored the position of her lips, her teeth, and even her tongue, Morgan knelt frozen in a stasis that was at first unbearable. She felt about to suffocate, to become violently ill. She tried to hold her breath, but the scent of green swamps was overpowering. As she breathed it in and let her tense muscles relax, the nausea passed and she was strangely, unaccountably, free of revulsion.

"Two," the Parthian child said perfectly.

"Three, four," she repeated after Morgan, her fingers still exploring Morgan's mouth.

Morgan was scarcely aware of it when Lurrp was replaced by another child, and still another. She didn't push them away, and she didn't get sick. Instead, she hardly noticed the smell and the touch for the immense, calm joy that filled her when she realized what was taking place.

The tactile-oriented children, once they could feel the sounds, had no difficulty imitating them. Morgan had put up every barrier, but when she surrendered, the eagerness of her pupils was inexhaustible. "Mother. Father. Tree. Water. What is your name?" The lessons over which she had labored so fruitlessly issued like echoes from the small throats.

The written letters were a greater challenge, but again Morgan took her cue from the children. She remembered the gummy paper wads.

No need to sacrifice her supplies for papier-mâché, though—not with a yard full of mud.

It was a bigger mess than she could ever have imagined, but after the children had formed an A of sloppy clay they didn't forget it. She was halfway through the alphabet when pleas to "feel my stomach empty" reminded her of lunch break.

But they could hardly have had time to eat, Morgan thought when they returned—they must have been too busy spreading the word. Her full complement of twenty-two students filled the room, all rambunctiously eager to catch up with their six lucky playmates. Morgan assigned the six as her aides, and the others learned from them.

At the end of the day Morgan ruefully surveyed her ruin of a classroom. She would get no points for keeping a trim ship, if Captain Kraskolin considered that important.

He didn't. Succeeding days unlocked the words that had been stored during Tiptin's bumbling tenure, and by the time Kras came the children had a working vocabulary. Some were even beginning to read.

"However did you do it?" the captain asked in open admiration.

When Morgan told him, he was even more amazed. "I would call that courage well beyond the call of duty. You know—the smell.

"By the way, would you mind if I open the door? It's still pretty strong in here."

"No—go ahead. I guess I forgot." She lied; she didn't smell a thing but fertile swamp, the rich smell of life.

"And God—what's this on your desk? Let me throw it out for you." Kras made a face and gingerly removed her latest *thrrup*.

Morgan smiled. He had a lot to learn about

Parth. But then, she had a lot of time to teach him.

   "You stayed on Parth for four years, I see," Billingsgate said.

   Morgan smiled dreamily. "Yes. They built me a house next to the school. It was the snuggest little place, even with the damp. My bed hung from the roof on lupod ropes that glowed in the dark." She winked. "To scare off the crawlers, you know."

   It hadn't scared off Kras, though, she remembered. How that bed had swung!

   The interviewer cleared his throat. "I can see that your experience on Parth was a positive one. No problems there. Let's move on to Roga, now. That must have been a different story."

   It was.

II. The Vampires Who Loved
Beowulf

"Morgan Farraday!" A shout pierced the noise and bustle of off-loading. At the terminal entrance a gaunt, past-middle-aged woman with short-cropped gray hair waved and beckoned.

Morgan hoisted her duffel and threaded her way around the containers and the knots of sweaty workers, trying to swallow her irritation. Appreciative comments followed the trim figure, but Morgan did not respond. Dr. Wheeler was two hours late, and the Lagos Port terminal was cold and drafty.

Not that she'd expected a big welcome. This was Roga, the dark planet. The vampire planet. The scrapings of the barrel, as far as Space Corps teaching posts were concerned. Morgan considered that she had every right to feel chagrined, especially after her triumph on Parth. On that planet Captain Kraskolin had had her instructing the other teachers, and here she wasn't even to be in charge of her own class. She was to be an assistant, as if she were a raw neophyte, or someone who hadn't made the grade on her own. And if the posting had been a disappointment, so was the assignment—teaching epic poetry to bat-creatures who couldn't even talk!

It wasn't Dr. Wheeler's fault, though, and Morgan had determined to keep an open mind about the *Alien Studies* author-anthropologist. But being kept waiting was a poor start, and when her new boss beckoned again, peremptorily, Morgan's irritation increased. However, she obediently quickened her pace.

"I'm Sarah Wheeler." A work-roughened hand gripped Morgan's, then propelled her hastily out of the terminal to an airsled parked on an edge of the rocket field. "Sorry for the delay. Minor emergency at the station—have to hotfoot it right back. No time to show you around town. Maybe later on. As you can see, there's not much here anyway."

She was right. It was a barebones port, with no frills. They were quickly airborne, Dr. Wheeler skillfully maneuvering over the blocklike buildings as she talked in staccato bursts. "Glad to have you here, Farraday. You come highly recommended. Surprised, though. I expected someone . . . older. But we'll see. Bit of an adjustment, in any case. Roga's not at all like Parth, you know."

"I know—I've heard the tapes." The airsled took on altitude as they passed over open country—flat dusty plains, low mountains in the distance, dark under the glowering sky whose heavy gray clouds never parted.

A cluster of rounded earth-covered roofs marked a Rogan underground settlement. It appeared deserted. "The Rogans don't like light even this dim?" Morgan asked. "They're all sleeping now?"

"That's right. I'm afraid you'll have to become a night owl too. No other way to teach them. At the station, you'll be on their time."

Strong winds buffeted the airsled, and Dr. Wheeler fought to keep it steady. They flew over more shadowy plains interspersed with what appeared to be marshes, and Morgan held onto her seat as they bounced roughly. Another underground city thrust upward like a long mole-hill.

They were almost to the mountains, which were higher now than they had seemed from a distance: purple cliffs hollowed by the wind. A single blinking signal light announced the approach to the Terran station-school.

The airsled banked steeply and descended to a feather-light landing. Dr. Wheeler was out in seconds, around to Morgan's side and unloading her gear. "That building straight ahead is our quarters. Sorry I can't get you squared away, but you'll find everything you need. The room on the left is yours. Expect you still feel rocky after entry, so why don't you rest?"

She unsnapped a key from a heavy ring. "Bolt the door after you. I'll be at the other building until dark. Hospital case."

She was gone, hurrying with great strides toward the smaller bubble-hut that squatted in the gloom of the overhanging cliff.

The station was sheltered, and the wind whistled harmlessly from beyond the bluff. Still, Morgan shivered. She unlocked the padlocked door and bolted it from the inside, disturbed by the tight security. Perhaps, she thought, the rumors about the Rogans were true. . . .

Morgan's room was spartanly furnished with a cot and worktable, but both were buried under a mass of papers, books, tapes, files, and even cartons of old clothing. Grimly she piled dusty boxes on the floor to make space for her own belongings. She knew that she was replacing Dr. Wheeler's husband, but he had been dead for six months and there would have been plenty of time to clear away his things.

Unpacked, she rummaged in the kitchen for a snack and then stretched out on the cot. She *was* tired, and in the gray light it was easy to pretend that it was evening.

When she awoke it was dark. Someone was pounding at the door, and she groggily stumbled up to let in Dr. Wheeler.

"You've slept? Good for you—I could tell you needed it." The gray-haired woman lighted lamps and the stove and filled the coffee pot. "Let's have breakfast. No—let me do it; I know where everything is."

She efficiently opened packets and heated and stirred, and had a hot breakfast on the table in minutes. When she sat down, though, Morgan could see the strain of an all-night vigil in her face.

"How is the patient?" Morgan asked. "And *who* is it? I thought we were alone here."

"It's a Rogan. One of my helpers. He met with an . . . accident doing some fieldwork for me. At the moment, there's a lot of unrest among the natives."

Dr. Wheeler stirred her plate of eggs, then looked up at Morgan with a worried frown. "I've been thinking about you, Farraday, and I hope you won't take it wrong if I suggest that you don't have to stay. You can catch the rocket out tomorrow. It's either that or be stuck here until the next one comes. I can get along alone; been doing it for six months."

Take it wrong! How else could she take it? Morgan choked on her coffee and sputtered. "Of course I'm staying," she finally said. "How would it look if I refused an assignment? Or are you refusing me?"

Dr. Wheeler stared at her hands. "No, I didn't mean that. It's just that—all right, I've never been one to mince words. This is a tough post, and I was hoping for someone with more experience."

She silenced Morgan's protest. "Oh, I know all about your brilliant success on Parth, teaching language. But we use the voder here, and I'm afraid the Rogans are a different matter entirely."

Morgan stifled her anger. She definitely was not leaving, but all the same she couldn't help wondering just what it was she would have to face. "Are they really . . . vampires?" she asked.

"I thought you said you'd been briefed," Dr. Wheeler said dryly.

"Of course I have." Morgan sat up very straight. "I just thought you could give me your personal observations. Or are your studies classified?"

"Not at all. But don't look to me to contradict the tapes. They're true. Yes, the Rogans are bloodsuckers." She said it matter-of-factly, as if she had said that they preferred bananas. "Greedy bastards, too. Several liters at a time. They feed twice a week."

Morgan tried to hide the effect of Dr. Wheeler's words. "But they have their own *jouk* herds, don't they? What I mean is, they aren't dangerous to us?"

Dr. Wheeler frowned. "What was on those tapes, anyway?"

"Nothing about their eating habits. It was mostly about their homes and cities and ranches —as much as we know, which is very little. And of course about their songs, since that's going to be my job."

The anthropologist snorted with disgust. "I should have guessed—don't give the sweet young things nightmares!" She looked at Morgan levelly. "Well, you'd better know now. Yes, they are definitely dangerous. If you provoke them, they'll suck you dry. And I mean *dead*, with no nonsense about transmogrification."

Morgan gasped. "I didn't know they drank human blood!"

"We didn't, either, but that's the way Nate died. My late husband." She paused, as Morgan sat in shocked silence, then tempered her revelation.

"It was his own fault, though. A freak occurrence, and not something that's likely to happen again."

She seemed very sure. "How do you know?" Morgan asked.

"One of the Rogans confessed. He was an aberrant, and they've taken care of him in their own way. And, as I said, it only happened because Nate was careless. Still, I had a devil of a time persuading the Corps to keep this station open, and only by swearing to be responsible for you. Now, are you still sure you want to stay?"

Morgan nodded, though she had to clasp her hands to keep them steady.

Dr. Wheeler arose. "Then you might as well meet your first pupils." She unbolted the door, and Morgan, close behind her, peered into the darkness at the black shapes huddled in a formless mass against the wall.

"They won't come inside unless you turn out the lights. But wait a minute—there's Far-darter, and maybe she'll come in to meet you. She's braver than most. Let me get the voder."

Dr. Wheeler returned with the voice coder and spoke into it. "This woman is your new teacher. Singer. She wants to see Far-darter inside. Please."

The voder transcribed the words into high-pitched squeaks, and a small dark figure detached itself from the others.

Inside, Morgan studied the female Rogan who crouched in the doorway. She was no more than a meter tall, with black leathery skin hanging loosely on a thin frame, generally humanoid in shape except for the webbed arms and clawed hands. The eyes in her bat-face were screwed tightly shut, but Morgan knew that they were red, as blood-red as the cruel small open mouth with the sharp protruding fangs.

The Rogan spoke into the voder—a thin, pierc-

ing wail that hurt Morgan's ears—and the translation issued in clipped impersonal computer
tones. "Welcome, teacher. Now we learn more
Earth songs. Happiness. We are ready, friends
and myself."

"Does she mean *now?*" Morgan turned in consternation to Dr. Wheeler. Surely she wasn't
expected to begin so soon.

Dr. Wheeler suppressed a faint smile. "No, I'll
send them away. Give you a few hours to pre-
pare. They're eager, you must understand. It's
been six months, and they were well into *Beowulf.*

"Come back midday," she said into the voder,
and led Far-darter out.

She looked at Morgan appraisingly. "Not exactly appealing, are they? Want to change your
mind?"

"No, I don't mind the way they look," Morgan
lied. "And I don't intend to provoke them." She
struggled to sound composed, when in reality
the sight of Far-darter had affected her most
unpleasantly. "I'm much more concerned about
having to use a voder to teach literature. Epic
poetry—that's really all they're interested in?"

"Nothing else. Nate tried to slip in some history and a little science, but they detected it
and boycotted him. Took him months to get
them back. You know the Corps rule—teach them
only what they ask for."

"I know, but poetry must come out sounding
rather . . . peculiar. And the vocabulary—is it
adequate?"

"Nate did a new coding for every epic. The
Iliad, Odyssey, Aeneid. His voder is still keyed
in for the *Beowulf,* so you won't have to do it.
Here, I'll get you all his files. No reason why
you can't continue where he left off—unless of
course you want to start off new with *Roland* or
Morte d'Arthur and a whole new vocabulary."

"No—no," Morgan said hastily. "*Beowulf* is

fine. I'm no literary scholar, and no voder expert, either." Dr. Wheeler had dumped a jumbled box of tapes and papers on the table, and Morgan began to sort through them.

Dr. Wheeler sat beside her. "Let me help. You have four hours before class, and I can show you what Nate was doing. His techniques, anyway —I'm not familiar with the material. All that was his department."

Dr. Wheeler seemed to have accepted Morgan, albeit grudgingly. They plowed their way through Nate's texts and notes until Morgan had a fair idea of what he had done and how she should continue.

She was impressed by Nate's scholarship. He could have worked from a modern translation, but he had made his own from the original Anglo-Saxon—just as he had done with the Greek and Latin epics. And for an audience that would neither know nor care.

Nor had his wife, apparently. Sarah Wheeler checked the voder memory banks for any new words, but the content she left entirely to Morgan. Fortunately, Nate had translated far ahead and it sounded good—Morgan didn't try to change it.

By lunch the two women were on a first-name basis—not exactly friendly, but a working relationship. Sarah had made it clear that she had her own research to pursue and couldn't be bothered with the teaching. Morgan would be in complete control there, and her pride was somewhat soothed.

Morgan heated soup while Sarah checked on her patient. She was back shortly. "He's gone," she said, "Damn it!—but I'm not surprised.

"They hate our surroundings," she explained. "He's far from well, but he'll probably heal better at home."

Morgan served. "What was wrong with him?" she asked.

Sarah was evasive. "A ... a hunting accident," she said. "Lost an arm. Nasty wound, but I did what I could for him."

Morgan pressed. "I thought it was some sort of trouble among the Rogans. 'Native unrest,' you said."

"Did I?" Sarah's weathered face became a mask. "Yes, they have their wars. We can't interfere. Whatever you do, don't try to get close to them. All I do is compile facts, and all you do is teach them poetry. We keep our noses clean and we're safe. Otherwise—you know what happened to Nate. He made the mistake of trusting a Rogan."

"But Nate's murderer was crazy, wasn't he? The others ..."

"Keep your distance with all of them!" Sarah snapped.

After a strained moment she offered a half-apology. "If I've frightened you, it's so you'll be prepared. You'll be all right as long as you don't overstep—but be sure to load your finger-needle. If you like, I'll stay with you this first time, just to help you get started."

Morgan was more than glad to accept the offer, and after lunch the two women packed up the voder and the notes and a couple of folding chairs.

Nate had held his classes outside, for the ease of the Rogans. Sarah led the way, surefooted in the darkness with only a thin beam of light.

Behind the station they climbed a stony rise that ended just under the cliffs. A rough basinlike amphitheater was already filled with the indistinct shapes of Rogans. Their shrill cries ceased abruptly as Morgan and Sarah came into view.

Someone had constructed a partially enclosed platform against the rock wall. "Nate used to recite from here," Sarah said, placing Morgan's voder on a large flat stone and her book and notes on another. "If you need to read you can shine a beam down here, without bothering them too much. Better not to, though. Nate always spoke from memory."

"I will, too," Morgan said. Sarah shut off her light, and in darkness Morgan unfolded her stool and faced the ranks of glowing red eyes.

These were adults, she knew, not the ingenuous children she had dealt with on Parth. They were, in fact, the elite of the clans, the singers: the repositories of Rogan myth-history, of the epic songs that were their art and music and literature. Morgan sensed their excitement as they waited for the new treasures that she would bring.

Nate Wheeler had made a spare, rhythmic translation which attempted to preserve the strong beats of the Old English line. It was the section in which Grendel's mother appeared:

> "To avenge her son
> She came then to Heorot,
> Where the Ring-Danes
> Slept in the hall."

The Rogans listened raptly as Morgan described the battle in the hall and the escape of the monster to the fenlands. She had memorized what she thought was a long enough passage, but even pausing after each line for the voder to translate, she was finished far too soon for her avid audience. They stirred and wailed, and Sarah whispered for her to continue.

She would have to read. Morgan switched on her beamer, and after a momentary flurry the Rogans settled down. She started with the description of the demons' lair:

"They that secret land
Inhabit, retreat of wolves,
Windy headlands,
Dangerous fen-path,
Where the mountain stream
Under the misty cliffs
Flows downward."

Morgan shivered, caught in the spell of the words. The gleaming eyes and dark shapes around her seemed transported, too. As she read on they began to sway almost hypnotically with the beat. It was a gruesome passage in which Beowulf accepted the new challenge, rode to the bloody pool, and found the severed head of the murdered thane.

Morgan's throat became raspy, and she stopped. "End for today," she announced. The chorus of answering squeaks sounded alarmingly like protests.

A wave of dark forms approached the stone podium, and Morgan rubbed her needle release uneasily. "Are they angry?" she whispered to Sarah.

But before Sarah could answer, a ghastly red mouth squeaked into the vodor. "Beautiful. Happiness. Many thanks," the machine voice translated.

One after another the singers expressed their delight and appreciation, then lifted their webbed arms and skittered off into the darkness.

"I'd say you were a success," Sarah said, helping Morgan pack up. "Feel better about it now?"

Morgan delayed answering until they were well down the slope. She had perplexing thoughts. "It went all right, I guess," she finally said. "An enthusiastic audience certainly helps. But you know, it wasn't really *teaching*. I could have been a robot out there—or even a tape recorder. Why does the Corps waste a trained teacher on something like this? Wouldn't it be more efficient to code the epics into Rogan speech and just give them the tapes?"

"Won't work," Sarah said. "The Rogans insist on a live teacher. It's their way. We tried the tapes, but they refused them. Insulted. Their singers have incredible memories, you know. Every word you said today they'll remember forever."

"And repeat it at their own songfests? Have you been to any?"

"No. Unfortunately, that's out of bounds for us."

They were back at the house, and Sarah made coffee. "So you've never heard the Rogan epics?" Morgan asked.

"Nate did. Some portion, anyway, from Fardarter. But she spoke much too fast for the voder, and all he got was a jumble about journeys and battles. He was trying to do a translation—it's somewhere in that mess he left. I've been too busy to go through it, I'm so far behind schedule with my own work."

Sarah's face settled into tired lines of discouragement. "The Corps is going to pull me out, you know, unless I produce a Rogan book soon. And in three years I haven't gathered enough information to fill a chapter."

"Because it's so dangerous to approach them?"

"Yes—that, of course. But what also makes it difficult for me is that they seem to have no sort of public lives. I've never studied sapients who were so reclusive. And since I can't get into their cities—wouldn't go alone, anyway—I've had to reconstruct from nothing but old bones and deserted settlements. Hardly the definitive study the Corps wants."

"What is it you're working on now?" Morgan felt almost at ease with this more human Sarah who could confide her own difficulties.

Sarah brightened. "On a ruined city I found just last month. Great luck—been going out there every day."

"When are you going again? Can I go along?"

Sarah frowned. The prickly shield was up again. "Frankly, I don't think you'll have time for sightseeing."

"But ... I won't be teaching eight hours a day."

Sarah gave her a look that shriveled any new hopes of intimacy. "I'm afraid you still don't understand the situation here. It may not be your idea of teaching, but it's no sinecure. When you finish the *Beowulf* and run out of Nate's translations, what then? You'd better have something ready—those Rogan singers won't want to be kept waiting.

"You'll find that you'll earn your credits at this post," she said crisply, getting up from the table. "We both will. And I for one can't be bothered with tourists." She started for her room. "I'll be off to the site as soon as it gets light, and you'll be sleeping. I'm going to bed now, and I suggest you get to work. Nate and I both found that there weren't enough hours in the day for all we had to do."

She closed her door and Morgan was left fuming, with burning cheeks. So Sarah Wheeler considered her a lazy dilettante, did she? An incompetent, compared to Nate. A nuisance who couldn't be allowed near her precious site.

Her first instincts about the woman had been correct. She was an anachronism—a dusty research machine with no humanity. Morgan had glanced through the two dull tomes that had established her reputation. Facts, statistics, measurements. Meticulous analysis, but with no feeling for the aliens she so painstakingly catalogued. No wonder she had been unable to establish any rapport with the Rogans. No wonder she had only dead cities to study.

Morgan glared at the closed door. Dr. Wheeler apparently wanted to see as little of her as possible—they would even have different shifts. In fairness, she admitted that the anthropologist needed light for her explorations while the teacher had to catch her students awake. But still—it was a good arranagement for two people who disliked one another.

At least, Morgan vowed, she would give Sarah no grounds to fault her half of the partnership. She washed the dishes from breakfast and lunch and sat down with her books.

She soon found that Sarah had been closer to the mark than she knew; preparing the next passage was no snap. Nate's translation ran out and Morgan sweated over an Anglo-Saxon dictionary and the battle with Grendel's mother until first light.

Sarah emerged from her room in full field gear. "I'm taking the airsled," she said. "You'll be safe here, but bolt the doors."

Morgan nodded and tried not to appear envious. Was she to see nothing of the planet?

Sarah unbent. "Maybe you can come tomorrow, if you aren't too tired." She took in the clean sink and the piled worktable and registered approval. "You'll be here a long time, you know."

At the moment it was small comfort to Morgan. She slept, and awoke to darkness and another performance under the cliff.

> "Then was by the hair
> Carried into the court
> Grendel's head,
> Where men were drinking
> Terrible to men,
> And the woman's also
> Wonderful spectacle
> Men looked on."

*   *   *

Morgan finished, stiff and dry-throated after two hours of recitation and reading. The Rogan singers had listened as intently as before, and again responded with high-pitched squeals of thanks. They began their exodus down the rubbly slope, excited and purposeful, and Morgan watched with wondering curiosity. Where were they going? Back to their burrows, to sing their own songs? To their *jouk*-herd farms? No public lives, Sarah had said. And their private lives shrouded in secrecy.

It was shameful, she thought, to know so little of them. To be so distant. She remembered Sarah's warning, but she also remembered her experience on Parth, where she had succeeded with the natives only when she had broken through her own prejudices. Sarah obviously hated the Rogans, after Nate's tragedy. But was she being fair?

She would have to make her own decision, Morgan thought. She detained one of the Rogans who was still squeaking thanks into the voder. The creature drew back, trembling, as Morgan touched the clawed hand. "Where do you go now?" she asked. "Can you stay to talk with me?"

The Rogan blinked and uttered a piercing wail. Morgan jumped, but just as she had stationed herself safely behind the podium another Rogan came flapping up and the frightened one disappeared.

"Far-darter," said the new arrival into the voder, identifying herself. "Talk, yes. All singers go home now. You like to come see?"

Morgan shrank from the glowing red eyes. But she was tempted. Sarah, with her standoffish attitude, had never been invited into a live city. What a coup it would be to beat the supercilious doctor on her own grounds!

"Talk first," Morgan said, hedging. She moved aside so Far-darter could share her platform. She placed the voder between them. No harm, she told herself, could come from a simple conversation. "Which Terran songs do Rogans like most?" she asked.

"Beo-wulf," came the voice from the voder. Far-darter shifted uncomfortably in the narrow space. She raised her arms and the hanging skin flapped. "Come *now*. You like to come now?" she repeated.

Morgan ignored the Rogan's impatience. "You have children, Far-darter?" she asked. "You have husband—mate? Teacher would like to know all about Far-darter. Be friends."

The Rogans grew even more agitated and uttered shrieks that the voder could not translate. She finally calmed. "Friends, yes. Teacher, Far-darter, friends. Teacher like to see Far-darter home? See song-hall?"

"Mor-gan!" A shout interrupted the conversation, and Far-darter cowered beneath the podium as Sarah approached with a light.

"Do not be afraid," Morgan said, silently cursing Sarah. "Doctor friend too."

Sarah switched off the light at Morgan's frantic pantomime, but not before Morgan had seen her grim face. The doctor arrived panting.

"Far-darter has invited me to visit their city," Morgan said, not bothering to disguise the triumph in her tone. "Maybe she'll let you come, too."

"Maybe you'd better have your head examined," Sarah said. She pulled Morgan roughly out of the enclosure. "You're all right?"

"Of course I am." Morgan struggled free. "Did you hear what I said? A chance to visit—"

"I heard. Yes, it's fine. Good. But let me handle it." She spoke into the voder. "Much thanks,

Far-darter. Doctor, teacher visit soon. Tomorrow. With Lagos Port men. Two. Is good?"

"Is good." Far-darter edged out of the enclosure. She raised her arms and started down the slope.

"Thank you, Far-darter. Friend. Goodbye," Morgan called after her. Then she turned angrily to Sarah. "Was it necessary for you to come barging in like that? We were just getting acquainted, and now you've frightened her off. I thought the class was supposed to be *my* province!"

"I was worried when you didn't return," Sarah said stiffly. They walked down the slope in silence, but Sarah registered disapproval with every motion of her rigid body. As soon as they entered the house she exploded.

"You don't listen, do you? I'll say it once more, and for your own good you'd better pay attention this time: in this post we aren't goodwill ambassadors. Between our species, that would be impossible—I've told you why. We need the base here, and they seem to need our stories. Strictly business, that's what it has to be."

"Are you so sure?" Morgan was fed up with Sarah's lectures. "Have you even *tried* to see the Rogans as creatures who have feelings, too? Maybe if they thought of us as friends . . ."

"Rubbish!" Sarah spat out rudely. "You seem to have become an expert rather quickly. And without much information." Her tone was icy. "Perhaps I should have told you more about Nate's death. He tried the same mistake as you— tried to get close to them. Tried to be friends. Yes, Nate was a true humanitarian. Would you like to know how he looked when I found him?"

Confusion gripped Morgan. "I . . . I don't think so."

"Wise. Since you can't avoid a certain amount of contact with them. But you *can* keep it to a minimum. And with safeguards. No solitary tête-à-têtes, no unscheduled visits to their homes. That's madness." Sarah sighed heavily. "As soon as I met you I was afraid of this."

"Afraid?"

"Yes. Of a know-it-all kid who wouldn't take directions." With that parting shot she stomped off to her room.

Sarah remained behind her closed door, and Morgan warred between embarrassment and defensive anger. After a while she tried to find relief by working on translations. She would finish the *Beowulf* in a few days, and had decided to attempt the *Kalevala* next. Nate had made a start on the Finnish epic, and it seemed like something that would appeal to the Rogans.

She thought about Nate Wheeler as she followed his careful scholarship, admiring the way he made the lines sing. He was something of a poet himself. A poet who had wanted to reach out to the Rogans beyond words, and had died for it.

Nate and Sarah. She tried to imagine them together—an unlikely couple, if ever there were one. Each must have been buried in his own world. Sarah knew nothing about the poems. "All that was his department," she had said in a tone of amused condescension. "That mess he left," she had called his overflowing files. "A humanitarian," she had said with bitterness. Her own desk and shelves were immaculate, and no one— human or alien—would ever pierce her iron guard.

But Sarah had been right. Nate was dead, and the flutter-headed young assistant had deserved her rebuke. Morgan was ashamed, though it didn't make her like Sarah any better. But something would have to give if they were to continue working together, and Morgan was prepared to do her part even if it meant eating humble pie.

Sarah had apparently done some thinking, too. When she joined Morgan for dinner/breakfast she was studiedly pleasant. "I'll take you out to the digs with me today," she offered, and Morgan just as civilly accepted.

They continued a restrained politeness during the flight, and at the ruined city Sarah's press of work and Morgan's absorbed interest pushed the remaining tension into a temporary limbo.

Two strong backs from Lagos Port named Nels and Ed and a crippled one-eyed Rogan composed Sarah's crew. The men were excavating the blocked tunnels while Sarah, with her Rogan guide, attempted to reconstruct the life that had once flourished in the underground complex.

Morgan followed them into rubble-choked black holes that had once been family quarters. In a larger cave, floor markings were revealed as the men dug out a layer of dirt. Sarah was busy everywhere with camera and recorder, and with her voder pumping the sorry-looking Rogan.

He gave her little information. "Song room," he said of the large cave, but would not elaborate on the ceremonies. "Sleeping place," he said of the smaller ones, but turned silent when Sarah questioned him about the details of family life.

"If I believed him, I'd have to conclude that the Rogans did nothing here but sleep and listen to the singers," Sarah complained.

"And fight wars," Morgan added. "Isn't that how this city was destroyed?"

"Yes, and our friend there, Twisted Foot, was one of the casualties. He says the last battle was only two years ago. Go up and look at the wall—or what's left of it. It's interesting; no other Rogan city has a fortification like it. And it's comparatively recent—much newer than the rest of the city."

Morgan climbed gratefully out of the dark

burrow into the gray light. She studied the leveled wall. It circled the underground city, but judging from the remnants it could never have been high enough to offer more than token protection. Two meters at the most. Hardly a high-walled Ilium, she thought, but still the comparison stuck. And the Rogans *were* familiar with the classical epics.

Sarah joined her on the wall, along with the workmen from Lagos. They ate a picnic lunch, and Sarah bribed the men into accompanying them that evening on Far-darter's promised tour of a live city. They were both reluctant, and she had to pledge a month's credits before they agreed.

Twisted Foot remained underground, afraid of the light. "Will he talk about the war?" Morgan asked.

"Not a word," Sarah said. "Apparently he was ostracized because of it. He was left for dead, but when he recovered he couldn't get back into the clan. Seems that his own people were responsible for the loss of his eye."

Morgan was electrified by a farfetched idea, and ran to the tunnel entrance. The Rogan was curled up asleep just inside.

"Fleet-foot!" she called into the voder. It was the name Nate had used for Achilles.

The Rogan was instantly awake, squealing and cowering against the wall. Morgan remembered Nate's translation of Polyphemus, the Cyclops. "Giant One-eye. That is you, too," she said.

The Rogan's terror seemed to confirm it.

A theory was beginning to take form. Too nebulous yet to tell Sarah, but definitely something to investigate.

The men, Ed and Nels, wanted to return to Lagos Port for additional weapons before embarking on the evening expedition. Sarah agreed, and they cut short the work day. They were to meet at the station that night after the lesson.

Sarah landed the airsled two kilometers from the Rogan city and they hiked in. Fortunately the wind was at their backs. Far-darter led, skimming lightly over the ground with bat-arms raised. The humans had to trot to keep up, the heavy-bodied men with curses and labored breaths. They passed a fenced-in field, and Sarah shone her beamer on a dark form fastened to the hump of a bellowing *jouk*.

Far-darter swooped back, shrieking, and Sarah shut off her light. They walked in darkness in a tight group. All were armed and Nels had a radio beamed to Lagos Port, but still Morgan felt frighteningly vulnerable.

Inside the city it was worse: close and stuffy and claustrophobic with the sense of too many bodies crowded into too small a space. The complex seemed to be filled with activity, but Morgan could see very little, even with the dim light that Far-darter permitted. The Rogan led them through a warren of passages that opened into cavelike rooms packed with dark forms. In the tunnels streams of Rogans skittered past them, and shrill cries echoed from the walls and assaulted Morgan's eardrums until her head throbbed in pain.

Far-darter led them into a large central room, mercifully quiet and empty except for a few workers who were laying stones in a corner of the rough floor. Sarah moved at once to watch them, but Far-darter pulled insistently at Morgan and she followed to an opposite wall.

The Rogan squeaked and fluttered and pointed upward, and Morgan held out the voder.

"Up. Look up. See," Far-darter said, and Morgan shone her beam high on the wall.

A withered black arm hung suspended from a frame.

Far-darter danced with excitement and shrieked into the voder:

> "The hand. The arm
> There was together
> Grendel's grasp
> Under the high roof."

Far-darter looked up at Morgan expectantly, but when Morgan only stared at her in increasingly comprehending horror she backed off.

Morgan ran to Sarah. "I think we'd better go."

Sarah was absorbed with her camera and waved her away. Nels, though, had been receiving from Lagos Port, and the message galvanized him to action. He pulled at Sarah roughly. "We're getting out of here *now*. I'll explain later."

Far-darter led them out, looking back at Morgan and fluttering and squeaking in what was either consternation or scolding—the voder could not translate it for all the other noise. She left them outside, and it was Sarah, not Morgan, who thanked her. Morgan was still trying to assemble her racing thoughts.

"There's been trouble at Lagos," Nels said as they fought their way against the wind back to the airsled. "A man killed. Work of the Rogans, for sure."

He didn't reveal the details until they were safe in the air. "Beheaded. Hacked off. And the head is missing."

Sarah swore, but Morgan wasn't surprised. Her theory was rapidly becoming fact. "Look in the marshes," she said. "Chances are you'll find a bloody pool. If the head isn't there, it'll turn up soon in Heorot."

"Heorot? What are you talking about?" Sarah

looked at Morgan as if she were a candidate for a straitjacket.

"The Rogans' Heorot—that big room we were just in. I'll explain it all when we get to the station—I'll need my notes."

"Listen to this description of Grendel's hand," Morgan said. She sat at a table spread with Nate's annotated translations.

> "In front of each (finger) was
> Instead of nails
> Most like steel
> The heathen's hand-spurs."

"Sure, it could be a description of a Rogan's clawed hand," Sarah agreed, "but what are you leading up to?"

"To the fact that the Rogans *act out* their epics. They're a degenerated race, and their own history is probably a constant repetition of their songs. You were right, Sarah, when you guessed that they do little but sleep and sing. Add to that—re-create."

Sarah nodded thoughtfully. "No life patterns that I could catalogue."

"Because they have none. They're actors. Imitators. Imagine their delight at getting some new material from us. The *Iliad*. The *Odyssey*. Plenty of bloody action there, and I'm sure they performed it all."

"And we thought it was just tribal wars!"

"No reason for you to suspect otherwise," Morgan said, "since the Rogans took all the roles. But the *Beowulf*—that was different. No wonder they loved it—to them, Grendel was clearly a Rogan.

"Unfortunately for us, though, the *Beowulf* had too many roles for humans. You didn't tell me exactly how Nate died, but was it anything like this?"

> "He quickly seized
> The first time
> A sleeping warrior
> Slit without warning
> Bit his bones,
> Drank blood from his veins,
> Swallowed huge pieces . . ."

Sarah's face was set and white. "Yes," she breathed, "that was it exactly."

"I thought so," Morgan said. "Nate made a notation here, by that passage. 'Tremendous excitement.' Apparently too much for them to contain."

"Then—that 'confession' was just a ruse. They were acting out the poem when they killed him."

"Yes, and they still are. Because they feel such an affinity to the *Beowulf*, they can't even wait until it's finished. I read about the murdered thane at my first session, remember? And they've already done that scene—head and all."

Sarah was speechless for a long minute. "Then what else do we have to look forward to?" she finally asked. "What other gruesome material have you fed them?"

"Too much. But luckily, passages that only concern violence to Grendel's mother, whom they see as one of themselves. So the next headless body should be a Rogan. Maybe the poor wretch who played Grendel and lost his arm, if he's still alive. Or Twisted Foot, who seems to get the bad roles, too."

"God, I hope you're right. But what about later? We can't stop giving them epics; there's our contract."

"Oh, I'll continue, but I'm certainly going to change my type of material. Not the *Kalevala*, or any more primitive sagas. No, the Rogans will have to go in a new direction, and it's something Corps Central will have to decide. I don't want the responsibility of guiding their future."

"It certainly opens up all sorts of possibilities," Sarah agreed. "And you're right—it's no longer a simple literary problem. We'll get a message off from Lagos in the morning. But until we hear, what will you do for the next classes?"

Morgan had already thought about it. "I'll end *Beowulf* quickly: an edited version. Then I'll give them something innocuous. *Hiawatha*, maybe—just the pastoral parts. They might even learn to smoke peace-pipes."

"That sounds safe enough." The tension was gone from Sarah's face. "At least, we won't have to send for a rescue rocket."

"No, we should both be able to finish our work."

Sarah looked her question, and Morgan continued: "Your book, I mean. Thanks to Nate, you'll find a wealth of material if we can finish translating those Rogan epics."

"Well." Dr. Wheeler had no more words. Her thoughts, however, were plain. She drew squares on the tablecover with her finger, then lifted her gaze to a spot somewhere beyond Morgan's left ear. The color came and went in her face. "Morgan, I . . ." She cleared her throat.

"Don't say it." Morgan couldn't allow Sarah to humble herself. She continued quickly: "You didn't misjudge me. I *was* a know-it-all, and if you hadn't rescued me from Far-darter that time, the murdered thane would probably have been *me*."

The thought, added to the stress of the last hours, caused Morgan to shudder. Sarah covered the trembling hand with her own. An inconsequential gesture for anyone else, but coming from the doctor it touched Morgan profoundly. Perhaps, she thought, the year would not be entirely without the comfort of friendship.

*   *   *

"So I got out of that one all right," Morgan finished. "Sarah and I left Roga together, and I spent a year with her here on Central, helping her with her book."

"Yes, I see that she acknowledged your contributions." Billingsgate shifted in his chair. "Are you getting tired? I could send for coffee."

"No, let's keep on with it." From the window, Morgan could see the sweep of the station rim curve and part of the docking arm with its grid of gantries. She longed to be out there, escaping from this artificial world on one of the silvery ships that hung there like bright promises.

"Good." The Corps officer fingered his wispy mustache as he consulted one of the readout sheets. "Your third assignment was to the Centauri Asteroids. Two years. Tell me about it."

She grimaced. "A rocky waste. Domes and suits. Definitely no place for children."

"Hmm. I notice that you recommended the belt be closed to dependents."

"Have they done it?"

"Uh . . . I'm not sure." Billingsgate swung around to his console and hunched over the keys. The screen came to life. "Yes, it's a restricted work zone, now."

He turned back to Morgan. "And Ophiuchi Frontera? You went there next, I see. What was it like?"

"Better, but still no picnic. Steamy jungles and simian aliens."

He studied her file again. "I see your friend Kraskolin was stationed there, too."

"With his new wife. It was . . . an awkward situation."

"I can imagine. That's why you only stayed a year?"

She nodded. "I jumped at the chance to go to Hedron II. A well-run military base, I was told. A temperate climate and human students."

"You were misled?"

"No not exactly. But there were surprises."

III. Cold War on Hedron II

Morgan spun and faced her pursuers. They hulked huge and dark, advancing in a ragged line through the half-light of the forest. She heard the rasping growls that in most ursinoids preceded blood-frenzy, breathed a prayer, and pressed the release of her finger-needle.

Holding up both hands, she walked slowly forward. If the urroks thought her unarmed, they might allow her to approach close enough. . . .

She was barely six meters from the band when she saw the hurtling ax blade. She ducked, then leaped forward to jab her steel-tipped digit into the hairy stomach of the foremost brute.

It went down, its cry choked by the paralyzing serum. She struck again and again, hoping fear would halt the attack before her needle emptied and more axes were thrown.

She almost succeeded. The urroks fell back, apparently bewildered by her uncanny power. Morgan sucked in great gasps of air and moved backward with what she hoped was godlike dignity.

It had been too close, though. Her legs betrayed her, and when she stumbled the spell was broken. She heard the enraged cries and saw the second flying ax as she knelt helpless.

Something struck her from behind, a heavy

mass that knocked her to the ground. I'm still alive, was her last conscious thought.

She awoke to the Suka shaking her. It squatted over her, its epicanthic eyes narrowed to slits, its lipless mouth lost in the overlapping folds of mottled brown skin. Beyond the Suka's face her vision swam in a blur of green leaves.

She sat up, closed her eyes, and pressed exploring fingers to her temples and eyelids. When she looked again the scene was back to focus: knobby trees, a dim glade, and the sprawled bodies of half a dozen urroks. An ax was stuck in the trunk behind her, and the Suka, squatting in its froglike crouch, bore with stoicism an oozing patch on its left shoulder. Its face was still flat and blank, the features covered by skinflaps.

They fold up their faces when they're worried or frightened. Morgan recalled the orientation slide lecture of Jarvis O'Connell, the base xenologist. *There's a characteristic movement of that loose skin for every nuance of emotion. Even if you can't understand the Suki speech, you can get some idea of what they're thinking by reading their facial muscles.*

She hadn't been able to master the deep-throated guttural sounds, though in this assignment, teaching service brats in the base school, it didn't matter. Only Jarvis among the Terrans had acquired oral communication skills, but still they managed to get along with the native sapients.

Morgan smiled and got to her feet to show that she was unhurt. "But you . . ." She pointed to the bleeding ax-graze wound.

The Suka's face relaxed, allowing its eyes and mouth to appear. Only the twitching fold above the now-exposed brow ridge betrayed a continued tension. The triangular eyes swept the motionless urroks, and from the tubular mouth orifice issued a series of grunts and croaks.

When Morgan did not respond, the Suka pointed first to Morgan's watch and then pantomimed the awakening of the urroks.

Her rescuer was familiar with the effects of the drug, Morgan thought with surprise. And with the function of her timepiece. She indicated a half hour on her dial; then, not knowing if the Suka understood, tried to approximate it by a hand motion of Hedron sinking.

She did not need the Suka to remind her that she was in trouble. The red sun was nearly below the tops of the trees, and she had no idea how far she was from the base. She had intended to be back from her visit to the wildlife tower well before dark, but that was before she had lost the trail and been ambushed. Now, the urroks she had stunned would awaken soon, and others might be lurking in the forest. The only other way to the Terran camp was by way of the firmax swamps which only the Suki could traverse with safety.

The Suka straightened from its crouch. Upright, it came to Morgan's shoulder—a thick-bodied figure with stalky legs and tiny thin arms. It moved off into the trees and returned, repeating the procedure when Morgan did not immediately follow.

It seemed to be offering to guide her. Morgan expressed agreement, but first offered to dress its wound from her field kit.

The Suka refused, moving off again. The blood had coagulated, Morgan saw, and the wound did not appear to be deep. The creature croaked and waved its arms, clear in its urgency to be gone, and Morgan followed.

They stayed at first in the trees, skirting the fingers of swamp. The Suka's bare splayed feet were sure on the mossy humus that caused Morgan's boots to slide. Its torso was partially wrapped in a wide belt dangling with wood and metal implements and variously shaped pouches. The Suki had no external sex organs, but Morgan guessed this one to be male—the females were generally taller, almost her own height.

Not even Jarvis knew much about them. While the Suki tolerated the Terran base, as well as that of the rival humans from Ceti Sector, they kept to their swamp islands and limited commerce to the minimum necessary for trade.

Morgan had felt the tension on Hedron II from the moment she had stepped off the shuttle four months ago. The guarded camp, the regulations, the constant fear of what the Cetians might be doing—she had never lived on such an edge. Terrans and Cetians maintained a shaky truce on the independent planet, erstwhile enemies willing to go to any lengths to ensure a steady supply of the antiplague drug firmax. The two camps talked cooperation while secretly arming themselves, and the Suki worked their firmax paddies and discouraged all visitors.

Jarvis would give up a month's credits to be in her place now, Morgan thought. He would be pumping her guide mercilessly. She knew that she should be gathering information for him somehow, but all she would be able to contribute would be a description of a mottled back and the stump of a vestigial tail.

The Suka quickened its pace and Morgan gave up her regrets about not being able to converse; she could barely keep up. As the trees thinned, the last low rays of Hedron shone in her eyes, and even when she tipped her visor forward she looked into a blinding red haze.

The Suka stopped and addressed her, rolling its face in wavelike undulations. Morgan wiped her eyes and saw the swamp ahead: masses of

reeds, scattered clumps of twisted trees and dark
patches where the moss riffled sluggishly.

Morgan walked with precision in the Suka's
footprints, the buzzing swamp noises and the
heavy smell of firmax a constant warning of the
ooze on either side. She caught a glimpse of
long stilted structures on higher ground, but
dared not raise her eyes from the path to study
them.

After a half hour they came to solid ground
again, and through a fringe of trees they emerged
on the edge of the savannah. The stockade of the
Terran camp rose in the distance.

Morgan and her companion approached an
enclosed group of log and stone and prefab buildings, mushroomed over the years from the simple receiving station agreed upon with the Suki
to a sprawling military complex of thirty acres
that tried to masquerade as a peaceful, low-tech
research facility. The Cetian base to the northeast was out-of-bounds to Terrans, but Morgan
understood it was just as extensive, spreading
almost to the plateau of the urroks. A stretch of
forest and swamp separated the two camps, and
behind them loomed the round-topped mountains that marked the limits set by the Suki for
human habitation.

A perimeter lookout waved Morgan and the
Suka on, and at the stockade gate more anxious-
faced guards hustled them inside. "She's here!"
one of them shouted.

"Thank God! We were about to send out a
search party." Arnie Vernor, the security chief,
rushed up, trailed by Jarvis O'Connell and a
medical team.

"I'm okay," Morgan reassured them. "But see
to the Suka."

"Why didn't you send a helex?" Arnie scolded.
A deep furrow bisected the brow of his wide,
square-jawed face. The security chief was a mus-

cular six feet four, formidable in an anger that Morgan knew was caused by his concern. "Drake says you left the tower at noon. Where the hell've you been?"

"I decided to detour through the woods to get some holos of those knobby *supsa* trees. I had plenty of time, and a baby could follow that trail.

"That is, until today," she amended. "Someone's moved all the markers. I nearly waded into the swamp, and when I backtracked around it some ax-wielding urroks attacked me."

"Axes!" Jarvis turned to her with a start. "Are you sure?"

"Of course I am; I almost got one. The Suka did."

"I can't believe it." Jarvis shook his head slowly. "From everything I've seen, they're only borderline sapient, and they've never used tools."

"It appears you haven't seen enough," Morgan said.

The xenologist stiffened. "I ought to know. I've watched them on their plateau for days at a time, and they've never exhibited the slightest degree of aggression. In fact, even when they sighted me they were indifferent."

"Well, they certainly weren't indifferent to me." Morgan didn't care to pursue the matter. The young scientist was on his first assignment, and defensive. He was a small man with flaming red hair, and as sensitive about his professional skills as his freckled skin was to the ultraviolet emanations of Hedron. He still wore his outside costume: completely shielded, from gloves to broad-brimmed hat. He had gone about half naked when he had first arrived, trying to gain acceptance by the Suki, but even with tannin shots he had gained only the scars of carcinomas.

"The urroks couldn't have moved the markers, either," Jarvis said. "They haven't that much cunning." He glanced at the Suka, who was quietly receiving a gel-spray on its wound. "Maybe it was one of them."

"But that one was almost killed rescuing me," Morgan said.

The Suka turned its head, and Jarvis jumped. "Impossible," he muttered. "They couldn't understand . . ." He faced the Suka and spoke clearly, in Terran: "How does the shoulder feel now?"

The Suka rippled the fold framing its ear cavity and croaked something in Suki.

Jarvis's color returned to normal. He repeated the question in Suki, and while he and the native were engaged, Morgan moved with Arnie into the gatehouse office.

She sank gratefully into the proffered chair, but her thoughts refused to rest. She mused aloud: " 'Barely sapient, no tools, and nonviolent.' How could Jarvis have been so wrong?"

Arnie rubbed his chin. "Maybe he wasn't. Maybe something else has been going on."

"Tampering? Surely the Cetians wouldn't dare. Or the Suki—they wouldn't unleash a menace on their home territory."

Arnie paced the narrow room. "Morgan, I don't know what to think. This ax—could you find it again?"

"No way. I couldn't even have made my way back if it hadn't been for the Suka. You could ask it—or him, or her. I'm afraid I don't even know which it is. And you know, I haven't even said proper thanks." She rose and started for the door.

Arnie stopped her. "Jarvis will take care of all that. Why don't you have a relaxing bath and meet me in—say, half an hour. After I've made my report to the old man I'll treat you to a backrub and a bottle of Elyrian *innis* I've been hoarding."

He grinned, and she smiled back. "You're on. My place—I'm sure I won't feel like going out again. But if I know the general, you'll never get away so soon."

"Wait and see. I know how to handle him."

Arnie's wink and the brush of his lips as they parted brought a warm glow to Morgan in spite of her fatigue. In the months she had been on Hedron II, Arnie Vernor had become both friend and lover. In most ways they complemented one another. With skin tanned and hair bleached by a dozen suns, he still preserved a sense of wonder that matched her own. If he had little interest in her antique books or her microfilm art collection, he more than made up for it by his steady strength and dependability. Arnie was one of the lucky ones who had found a vocational slot for which he was supremely well fitted, and the base and all who knew him profited.

Morgan envied him his quiet self-confidence. At thirty-two she would have liked to have shared it. Her own Space Corps teaching jobs had been a series of challenges, not all of which she had met to her self-critical satisfaction. Some, in fact, had defeated her. Still, she wouldn't have missed any of it—the adventure, the strange worlds, and always the children: the young minds like the enfolded Lurian *sclerilis*, opening layer after delicate layer to the one correct touch.

On Hedron II the challenge was not so exotic. Her students were children of the growing number of SEF officers who had long-term duty on the base. It should have been an easy assignment, no new culture to learn, but she had found the youngsters of rank and privilege harder to reach in a way than naked alien urchins. And with demanding parents to satisfy while saddled with the chafing restrictions of a military authority, she had come to depend increasingly on Arnie's supportive friendship.

Jarvis and the Suka were still standing by the gatehouse when Morgan left Arnie's office. She would be able to render her own thanks after all, she thought as she hurried to join them.

"His name is Grikkoor," Jarvis said when he had finished translating for her.

The Suka sent quivers through his raised cheek-folds; a sign, Morgan knew, that he was pleased. In his stacatto burst of croaks she could discern, with imagination, a crude rendering of her name.

Jarvis translated as precisely as he could. "Morgan Farraday. I am told that you are a great mother of the young of your species."

More folds appeared on Grikkoor's face, an oscillating network on either side of his mouth.

Morgan had to laugh. "No, a teacher. An instructor." To Jarvis: "Can you explain the difference?"

Jarvis tried, then turned to Morgan. "Mother-nurturer is a position of honor among his species. I don't know if he understands the concept of a school."

Grikkoor continued to ripple his face. He hunched his back and worked his slender fingers as if playing an invisible keyboard. He croaked again.

"He wants to observe your class." Jarvis said.

"The children? No, I . . . I couldn't possibly," Morgan stuttered. There was no telling how the sheltered diplomatic darlings, most of whom suffered from xenophobia to some degree or other, would react to a Suka at close range. Privately, she thought it might not be a bad idea, but she had her job to consider. "Why does he want to?" she temporized.

Jarvis ran a finger under his high collar. "How would I know? Probably it has something to do with their feelings about children. He still thinks you're some kind of a supermom." He frowned. "You owe him," he reminded her. "He seems to assume that you'll repay your debt. How can I tell him that you refuse?"

Morgan continued to stall. "But . . . the children aren't allowed visitors," she lied. "Tell him, though, that I'd be happy to show him the classroom, the equipment, the bookspool files. Any time. It can be arranged."

Jarvis translated, and the alien's face subsided into flat planes.

"Please," the xenologist begged. "If we could make a friend, it would mean so much to my work."

Morgan cast about for a compromise. "He could watch through a one-way glass," she finally said. "Ask him. See if that's good enough."

Jarvis did so, and Grikkoor responded by lifting his head and reanimating his face. Morgan knew his answer before Jarvis gave it: "It would give him extreme happiness."

Morgan suffered misgivings as she hurried to her quarters. While the official Terran policy was to placate the Suki in every way—after all, under the Free Worlds Charter they controlled their portion of the planet and doled out the firmax—unofficially the aliens inspired at best polite shudders among the high-ranking families.

It was a delicate dance, as fine as that between the Terran and Cetian camps, and Morgan feared tipping the scales in any direction.

But surely allowing Grikkoor into her classroom could have no political repercussions, she told herself. Not unless—she couldn't ignore the niggling worry planted by Jarvis—not unless the Suka had somehow engineered the "rescue" for precisely the end that he had gained.

Morgan's head ached. Jarvis would have to stay with the alien every second, she vowed. He was supposed to be an expert and he should be able to keep their guest in line.

She lingered too long in her bath, trying to soak out her tensions, and ended up rushing to be ready in time for Arnie.

Fortunately he was late himself. She had just slipped into a caftan and brushed the snarls out of her damp mop of thick, brown hair when he was at the door.

After a kiss came apologies. The meeting with General Cross hadn't gone according to plan, Arnie admitted ruefully. "He had me on the hotseat for giving you clearance to go to the wildlife tower, and of course he's upset about the sabotaged signs and the hostile urroks. He's sure the Cetians are responsible. We're sending for more troops immediately to beef up our security."

"More? How will we ever account for them?" Morgan did a fast walk through her studio room, picking up dirty boots and discarded clothing and throwing them into the closet. "We've so many troopers now disguised as botanists and technicians and groundsweepers and what-have-you that the Cetians have got to know we're way over our quota."

He grinned wryly. "Don't you think *they* aren't? That new ag station they built is swarming with strong-arm types. 'Agronomists'—hah! The Suki may be fooled by all this 'scientific' activity, but neither we nor the Cetians are that gullible. We may not be willing to rock the boat, either of us, but this is one base that's sure as hell going to be ready."

Morgan hugged her arms. "What's the word from home?"

"Last we heard, still a stalemate. We're both keeping to our sectors. Cross doesn't want to be the one to touch off the flare."

"So we go on holding our breaths." Morgan

accepted the squat brown bottle that Arnie ceremoniously presented, and searched her kitchen unit for glasses. She found two that had once held fruitbeads and absentmindedly polished them on her sleeve. "You know, those Cetians really don't deserve to get firmax if it's true about their starting the plague on Prantax Beta. The colony was nearly wiped out, I understand."

"I wouldn't believe that rumor about Ceti being responsible. They've accused us of germ warfare, too."

"Better watch it—you sound like a Ceti lover."

Arnie snorted. "No danger of that. I've seen their prisoners—or what was left of them."

Morgan shuddered. "And to think they were once a Terran colony."

"Our first." Arnie's voice sharpened into bitterness. "Tau Ceti III, the Great Adventure. If we had only known. . . ." He stared at a blank space on the wall until, rousing himself, he took the glasses from Morgan. "But that's enough gloomy talk. I promised you a relaxing evening, remember?"

The *innis* was honey-thick. Arnie held the bottle high and spun it while he poured, sending a swirling rope into the glasses. Morgan applauded when he cut off the stream at precisely the right moment.

"Ahah! About time I learned that trick." Arnie settled himself on the daybed and pulled Morgan down beside him. "You haven't told me yet about your visit to the tower. How was Drake? Still compiling his zoological encyclopedia?"

Morgan savored her drink in tiny tongue-laps. "Drake's worried." She formed a moue of apology; it was impossible to keep away from the one compelling concern. "He doesn't think the Cetians believe for a minute that we're really studying wildlife from up there. He's seen them skulking around, probably with lasereyes." She frowned. "Drake hates being a front for all those military and undercover types. That sweet old guy really *cares* about his research."

"It's one great observation platform, though."

"I know. It's probably necessary, and I don't mean to be critical." She snuggled against him. "I should just stay inside the camp and 'not worry mah pretty hay-ed.' "

"You've been talking to Miranda Cross."

"Half guilty. You know you don't talk to her; you listen. She cornered me in the mess yesterday and bent my ear off about her stepson and the way I've been hampering his career. According to her, Waldo could be teaching the class by himself."

Arnie didn't respond with the expected hoot of amusement. When Morgan looked at him questioningly, he shrugged. "Sure the kid's a pill, but you ought to try to get along with him. After all, his father—"

"Is God Almighty around here." Morgan sat up, shaking off his arm. She knew she shouldn't blame Arnie for not understanding her difficulties with Waldo, but all the same his attitude bothered her.

"No, I wasn't going to say that." Arnie said. "The general's okay, and you know it. We're lucky to have him here. It's just that it's a shame he has to deal with family problems, too. A son like Waldo and a wife half his age—I don't envy him his lot with that one, either."

Morgan raised an eyebrow. "Most men would disagree."

"Most *young* men. But he's pushing seventy.... Dammit, Morgan, you know what I mean!"

She rescued him. "Sure I do, but I still think the general's happier than he deserves to be. I met Waldo's mother at Cygni Station, and she's a lovely lady. A lovely *mature* lady. It's the usual sad story."

"I agree, I agree." Arnie set down his drink. "And that's enough about them." He began to knead her taut shoulder muscles. "I think it's time for that massage."

Morgan allowed herself to grow limp. She had intended to tell him about Grikkoor's request, but changed her mind. She wanted no more talk, only the soothing touch of his hands.

The base school was one room in the building that also housed the library and the chapel. Jarvis, who had been waiting when Morgan opened the classroom, only increased her nervousness by following at her heels as she prepared for Grikkoor's visit. "It could be a real breakthrough, if he decides to trust us," the xenologist reminded her. He checked the glassy panel that cut off one corner of the room. "Will he be comfortable enough in here?" A Suki squat-stool had been placed behind the screen, and Jarvis added a table. "I brought a plate of that swampweed they chew on, in case he gets hungry. And a glass of beer. They seem to like it." He came out of the enclosure and fiddled with the wall thermostat. "He'll be much too cold."

"Give him a blanket," Morgan said, resetting the control. "The kids will complain to all the gods of space if we have it that hot in here."

"What's going on?" Waldo Cross, Morgan's teaching assistant, slouched in the doorway, sipping from a steaming cup. He was elegantly dressed in a satin flight suit, his hair meticulously waved and his fingernails painted in rainbow colors.

A tantalizing aroma wafted into the room. Real coffee, Morgan recognized with a twinge of envy. But of course Waldo could afford such luxuries, she thought. His meager salary was probably as big a joke to him as his "assistance" was to her, but Daddy had created the post for him and she was stuck. Half the time he didn't show up, but it was just her luck that today of all days he would appear, and early at that.

However, it should be easy to get rid of him. "I won't need you this morning," she said. "In fact, why don't you take the whole day off? Jarvis and I are going to be doing some testing, and there's really nothing for you to do."

Waldo sauntered into the room. He finished his coffee and left the sticky cup on her desk. "Naw, there's nothing happening anywhere today. I'll hang around." He inspected the room in a leisurely fashion while Morgan squirmed. "What's that panel back there for?"

Morgan thought fast. "It's an . . . experiment. We're testing some new recording equipment, and I don't want the kids to know they're being monitored."

Waldo seemed to accept it. He turned to Jarvis. "How come you're in on this? Out of your line, isn't it? Or won't the froggies let you near enough to test them?"

"It's a . . . comparative study," Jarvis said. He made a show of busyness, rifling through a sheaf of printouts, but he couldn't keep from glancing at the clock. Grikkoor was already due at the gatehouse.

Morgan grabbed a list from her files and handed it to Waldo. "Fine. If you want to help, you can start out by getting these bookspools from the library." If he ran true to form, the trip next door would take him an hour. They could get Grikkoor installed and the class underway.

Waldo left, followed by Jarvis. The xenologist returned shortly with Grikkoor and settled the alien behind the screen.

"He's satisfied," Jarvis said to Morgan, "but what about me? I was going to stay in here with him, but now that you've made up that stupid story . . ." He glared. "What am I supposed to be doing? What's Waldo going to tell his father?"

"Stupid, eh? I didn't notice you coming up with anything better." Morgan was already regretting the plan, but it was too late. "I'll say that you're back here operating the equipment. I'd better lock you in now; the kids will be coming."

Jarvis pulled up a chair beside Grikkoor, and Morgan latched the panels into more or less immovable position. "Please be quiet back there," she warned, then opened the door to the first students.

Morgan had a class of thirty-five, from six years old to sixteen. Even with the disparity of ages it would have been manageable, with an able assistant. They were bright youngsters, and she should have been able to expand their mental horizons as well as ground them in basic compuskills.

But not with Waldo.

Waldo knew more than she did about everything connected with education. "Why sweat over these" he had said when she had ordered history spools. "Boring. The kids can learn all that on sleeptapes." When she had tried to organize discussions on the spools, he had refused to participate. "Who cares about that old crap?" Since he was a role model, her discipline suffered. And worse—she had to rely more than she liked on the rote learning of the sleeptapes and the teaching-machine programs.

When Morgan's first group arrived, the eight-to-ten-year-olds, she got them busy immediately at the machines with sleeptape reinforcement. This left her free to give personal attention to the next group, the youngest ones, who were reading at a variety of levels. No one commented on her explanation about the screens.

The older kids straggled in, claimed their com-

puter turns, or wasted time in various ways
while waiting. Waldo returned with the bookspools and Morgan tried to inspire interest, but as
usual he sabotaged her.

"So what's been happenin', keeds?" Waldo
straddled a chair facing the group of teenagers
and prepared to gossip. "Hey Leila, late night,
eh?"

Leila Provo, a sixteen-year-old with a wom-
an's body and great dark eyes, stifled a yawn.
She ignored Waldo and selected a Spaceways
Romance, over which she promptly fell asleep.

Morgan watched her, troubled. Leila showed
the most promise of any of her students—her
test scores were well in the Academy range—
but lately she had only been occupying space in
the classroom. Her mother was comstat officer
for the base, a position that prevented her from
spending much time with the girl. Morgan remembered herself at the same age, pulled one
way by glands and another by ambition, and
tried to be friend as well as teacher.

It appeared now that the glands were win-
ning. Annalee Provo had complained to Morgan
about her daughter's late hours. She suspected
one of the troopers and had asked Morgan to
counsel the girl, but so far there had been no
opportunity.

Leila slept on, oblivious to Waldo's loud teasing. He finally leaned over her and whispered
something which Morgan could not hear, but
which inspired raucous laughter from the rest
of the group.

Morgan's patience gave way. "Waldo, if you
can't be useful, at least be unobtrusive," she
snapped.

A mistake, she realized immediately. Waldo
straightened in offended surprise. "Unob—what?"

A couple of the kids snickered, and Waldo's
mouth tightened.

"It just means to be less distracting," Morgan said. "Why don't you see if anyone in the spelling group needs help? Or take your break—it's nearly time."

He wasn't mollified. "You seem to be awfully jumpy today. I wonder why. Could it be . . ." He turned and studied the panels.

Morgan felt herself flush, then turn cold. Waldo saw, and grinned gleefully. "I wonder just what *is* going on in that corner." He stood and walked toward the screen, every gaze in the room following him. He would get his revenge, she knew with a sinking sick dread.

He knocked on the screen. "Hey, Jarvis, you in there? How about letting us see what you're doing."

When there was no response he pried open the latch and slid aside the panels.

Waldo's amazed whistle hung loud for a moment, then was drowned in a chorus of screams. "Wait, wait, it's all right, there's nothing to be afraid of," Morgan shouted, trying vainly to halt the stampede for the doors.

Grikkoor sat immobile, his face a folded mask, and Jarvis looked ready to faint. "Just wait until I tell my father!" Waldo whooped, following the last of the children from the room.

"A Suka in the classroom? You actually exposed those impressionable children?" General Cross's face was stony except for a single throbbing vein on his temple. "Whatever can you have been thinking of, Farraday? I thought we were getting an experienced, reliable teacher, but it looks as though I've been misled."

The general sat stiffly behind a shining expanse of desktop. His fingers drummed on the surface. "Inexcusably poor judgment," he said in conclusion. "And it certainly will appear in my final evaluation. Have you anything further to say? Either of you?" He turned his accusatory gaze from Morgan to Jarvis, who had shared in the dressing-down.

Jarvis gulped and shook his head. Morgan couldn't think of anything more to say, either. The general had dismissed her stumbling explanation of a debt repaid as "precipitate" and "ill-advised," with Jarvis being accountable for the latter.

The teacher and the xenologist had never ranked high in the estimation of the general, Morgan knew, and now his distrust of nonmilitaries would seem to have been justified. She wished she dared point out that if the children had been allowed more exposure to the non-threatening life forms of the planet they would not have reacted so irrationally, but it was certainly not the time to criticize policy. Especially when it was *his* policy. So she clamped her lips and studied the toes of her boots and waited for the ordeal to end.

"In that case . . ." The general had risen to terminate the interview when a loud knock on the door froze all three.

Annie burst in, waving a hand in apology. "Sorry to interrupt, sir, but there's trouble at the tower. I just got a call from Drake. An armed squad of Cetians showed up and demanded the right to an immediate inspection. He had to let them in. I'm heading over there now in the airsled, with a dozen men."

The general was galvanized. "What's the status there now?"

"Don't know—we can't raise them."

"Damn! If they find that equipment . . ." General Cross and Arnie hurried out together.

Morgan stared at Jarvis, her humiliation forgotten. "We all know what was in that tower."

Jarvis, still smarting, shrugged and did not answer.

"Jarvis, snap out of it," Morgan said. "Cross isn't concerned about us anymore. We've all got more important things to worry about."

Jarvis's mouth still drooped, but he made an effort to respond. "So what if the Cetians have found out that we've been spying? They've probably got their own agents right here in the compound."

"An astute observation." General Cross was back, with two guards. His jaw was set grimly. "Lock her up," he ordered, pointing to Morgan.

At first she was too shocked to protest, but when the men seized her by the arms she set her heels and refused to budge. "At least tell me what this is all about," she insisted. "None of those kids was hurt."

The general glared. "Thanks only to Waldo. But what about the men at the tower? You *were* there yesterday, weren't you? You seem to have a genius for attracting disaster." He switched his anger to the guards. "I said get her out of here!"

Morgan was dragged out of the headquarters building, hustled through the compound at double time to the lockup, and deposited in a bare holding cell.

She saw no one for three hours, alternately fuming and brooding. The rank injustice, she seethed, when her only concern had been to help Jarvis in his research. And he, the little weasel, was probably sucking up to the general and telling him it was all her idea!

As she reviewed her situation she realized how bad it looked. First the visit to the tower, then the long delay on the way back—plenty of time to have rendezvoused with Cetians and Suki both, to have concocted a ridiculous story of ambush and arranged admittance for a curious alien who might for all they knew be a Cetian spy.

And Arnie, who might otherwise have helped

her, was at the very moment facing armed Cetians, perhaps engaging in a skirmish that might touch off a war.

She shivered and hugged her knees, perched on one edge of the cot that was the room's only furniture. The lockup was constructed from native stone, impervious to Hedron's rays. A high slitted window admitted faint light, and in the black-shadowed corners of the cell she heard skittering movement.

Finally a guard came—Hanni Szi, whom she knew—and moved her to a more comfortable room. Hanni was apparently under orders not to talk, but she relented enough to give Morgan a sketchy report. "There have been some casualties, and Arnie's on his way back now. We're all on alert status."

She hurried off, ignoring Morgan's pleas for more information. The lunch and dinner hours both passed, with Morgan apparently forgotten. She paced, demolished her fingernails, tried unsuccessfully to nap, and fretted some more. It was completely dark and she had at last fallen into an uneasy doze when the door opened and a light awakened her.

"Arnie!" Her words tumbled out in a rush. "You're all right! What's happened? I've been in here all day, and ... General Cross thinks ... there was something in the corner ..."

Arnie's clothing was sweat-stained and his face was etched with tired lines. "I'm sorry about this, but you're free now. On my charge—Cross still has reservations. Morgan, why didn't you tell me about that Suka?"

"Later. The tower. I haven't heard a thing. What happened out there?"

He breathed a deep sigh. "The Cetians have closed the tower. They must have had inside information about the scanners and probes—they knew just where to look. Found our cache of arms, too. They claim we've violated our treaty and they're taking it to the Suki."

"Hanni said there were casualties."

He took her hands. "Drake. The Cetians released all the others."

"But . . . Drake wasn't even a trooper."

"It seems he foolishly tried to keep the Cetians out of the armory."

"And you couldn't do anything?"

"They were entrenched by the time we got there. It would have a taken a full-scale attack to dislodge them, and of course the general couldn't risk it."

"So Drake is dead, they've got the tower, and we just sit here." Morgan jerked out of his grasp. She knew that her bitterness was unjustified, that Arnie had to obey instructions, that none of them wanted to set off the tinderbox.

But Drake, who had never harmed the least living creature. . . . She wept out her frustration.

Arnie held her, and his comfort eased her. "Let me take you to your room," he said when she was in control again. "I'm sorry about your being locked up like this, but Cross is wild to find a scapegoat and you seem to be it."

"He still thinks I'm a spy?"

"I couldn't convince him otherwise. He has no proof, though, so you're free as long as you don't leave the base."

She shrugged. "Where would I go, anyway? I'll be okay as long as I'm out of here and can get back to my work."

"There's more, I'm afraid." Arnie bit his lower lip. "I hate to tell you."

"Well?"

"You've been barred from the classroom, until we get this straightened out."

"But . . . who's going to teach? Surely not Waldo!"

He nodded, watching her warily.

She choked off the bitter protest. What would be the use? "Don't worry, I'm not going to explode," she said. She didn't even want to think, now. "Let's go by the mess and grab a sandwich—what kind of a guest house are you running here, anyway? Did you know they don't even feed the prisoners?"

Morgan chattered determinedly as they located a snack, and kept it up while Arnie walked with her to her quarters. To the few people they met she put on a show of nothing being wrong, pretending not to notice the hostile stares from those whom she didn't know well and the embarrassed glances from the ones she had considered her friends. It was a strain, though, and she finally closed her door with relief.

Alone, she gave up the facade. She couldn't remember when she had felt so angry and helpless. She had been in tough scrapes before—had faced bloodthirsty aliens and survived on scorching and freezing and rain-sodden planets—but the threat had never been to her character.

Barred from the classroom. Unfit. Cross's accusations burned like a disfiguring brand.

Morgan wasted a half hour on self-pity, on "how could he's" and "if only's," before stubbornness rescued her. She would fight in the only way she could—by finding the real spy. It was her one chance to save her reputation and possibly the base itself.

Two hundred troopers, and half that many officers and dependents. Where could she begin?

She tried to think logically. It would have to be someone with a degree of intelligence, freedom of movement, and motive. That would seem to eliminate most of the troopers, who were restricted to the base. She began to examine the other possibilities, and came up immediately with Waldo Cross. She knew she was not being strictly objective, but even barring her personal feelings Waldo was an apt suspect. He had both opportunity—access to the general's keys and to his files—and incentive—expensive tastes and an overweening thirst for any kind of power. He had shallow loyalties, if his irreverent comments in class could be taken seriously, and most telling to Morgan, he had done his best to discredit her.

The more she thought about it the more likely it seemed. General Cross had accused Morgan of snooping during her visit to Drake at the tower, but Waldo could have found the tower blueprints in his father's desk, with no necessity for a visit.

The next day she confided her suspicions to Arnie. He was too busy to allow her more than ten minutes of his time, but over coffee he listened and didn't immediately dispute her suggestion. "I can't do anything about it now, though," he said. "I'm tied up with the negotiations. You wouldn't believe the security."

"What's going on?" Morgan had heard nothing.

"Between us and the Cetians over the tower incident," Arnie explained. "The Suki are in on it, too. They want a new treaty and assurances of future peace or out we go, both camps. And it's got to be done today; the Suki aren't patient." Arnie glanced at his watch.

"I'm sorry; I won't keep you, then."

"No, it's okay." Arnie reached across the table and patted her hand. "I'm glad you're not sitting home—"

He stopped himself. He had been going to say "sulking," she was sure.

"Not letting this get you down. Tell you what— there'll be a reception tonight, to celebrate the new treaty. The Cetians and the Suki will send representatives. Miranda's planning it. You know, her usual bash. Come with me."

She was touched, but she couldn't let him put

his own job on the line by flouting General Cross. "No, I couldn't; not with this cloud hanging over me. Everyone seems to know—Waldo's probably shot off his mouth all over the base—and I can't stand the way people look at me."

"But that's why it's important to keep your head up. Not to give the idea that you've anything to be ashamed of. And if you're serious about getting the goods on Waldo, or whoever it is, you've got to get out and circulate."

He was right, and she changed her mind. They arranged to meet that evening, and Morgan spent a restless day, mostly in her quarters.

The few times she went out were ordeals. Three mothers from her Parents' Club looked the other way when she ran into them at the commissary, and she left with only half her order. Maybe with Arnie she could brazen it out, she thought, but not alone.

Outside, half running with a sack of groceries, she heard someone shout an expletive. The worst humiliation, though, was in passing her classroom. She couldn't resist a quick glance through the window, and it was just as she had expected— the little ones playing in a chaos of disorder and Waldo ensconced in her chair with his feet on her desk, surrounded by his coterie of teenage admirers. Leila, she saw, was foremost in the group.

Morgan dressed for the party in a long filmy gown cut in the Elyrian style of draped panels. She had used a flesh-colored undersheath with it before, but tonight she wore it as it was intended—with her breasts clearly visible through the sheer fabric.

They were small, but firm and well shaped, and she had even painted the nipples. Miranda Cross, who was the fashion arbiter for the base, would not be able to accuse her of "provincial modesty" this evening, Morgan thought.

She was glad she had taken such pains when Arnie appeared in his dress silver and blues. "You look ... delicious," he said. "But I think I've just changed my mind about showing you off. There's no one on this rock deserves it."

"It's too late." Morgan took in all of his imposing spit-and-polish. "And you're not so bad yourself."

"Arnie!" She fended off a hand. "I've just spent an hour getting into this outfit!"

He accepted defeat. "Then let's go and give Miranda's guests an eyeful."

The mess hall was decorated with plants and flags and an elaborate buffet. It was already packed. Heads turned when they entered, but Morgan held herself proudly and smiled down the stares.

"What a suh-prize!" Miranda Cross exclaimed. "Ah wasn't expectin' to see *you*, Mah-gin." The general's young wife had slanting green eyes and blond hair that cascaded down her back. Her voluptuous figure was well displayed in a skin-tight jeweled *cheongsam*: demurely collared, but with a thigh-high slit in the skirt.

"I wouldn't dream of missing one of your events," Morgan said sweetly.

Miranda latched on to Arnie. "Ah need a strong man to he'p me. The ice machine ..." She bore him off, and Morgan joined a group that surrounded the two Cetian ambassadors. Resplendent in gold robes, they beamed and exuded good fellowship that was noticeably not returned. "The new treaty specifies unrestricted entry into both of our bases," the tall one was saying in almost perfect Terran. "There will be no more secrets. An equal distribution of firmax and peace under Hedron."

His words were received with silence.

"Friends of yours?" Waldo Cross walked by, with Leila on his arm. Morgan reacted to his insulting grin with a quick flush of anger, but she bit her tongue. Leila avoided eye contact and guided Waldo away.

"I . . . was really sorry to hear about you losing your job." Annalee Provo, dark and regal and softspoken, placed a hesitant hand on Morgan's arm. They moved to an unoccupied space behind Miranda's imported palm. "I want you to know that I don't believe for a minute those rumors about your being a spy. Leila doesn't either, though she wouldn't tell you so herself."

They both followed the progress of Leila and Waldo with worried eyes. "How long has that been going on?" Morgan asked.

Annalee sighed. "Frankly, I don't know. Maybe I was wrong thinking she'd been sneaking out to meet one of the troopers—someone I wouldn't approve of. It could have been young Cross all the time."

"You approve of Waldo, then?"

The older woman hesitated. "What can I say? Leila is far too immature to become involved in anything serious, but since she doesn't listen to me anyway I suppose the general's son is preferable to an uneducated mercenary."

Morgan felt surer than ever about Waldo. He had certainly gotten what he wanted, all around. Annalee went on about the difficulty of rearing children, and Morgan only half listened. She watched Waldo across the room, and smoldered. Annalee might be adept at reading helexes, Morgan thought, but she was certainly shortsighted when it came to her daughter's welfare. Waldo was poison for Leila.

Morgan pondered how to expose him. With the new open-access policy there would seem to be no further need for spying, so perhaps it had been a one-shot deal. If so, her case seemed hopeless. Unless . . . she could enlist Leila. She knew from the stance Leila had always taken during discussions on ethics that the young idealist would never countenance espionage for personal gain.

But as Morgan observed the couple giggling together, any hope of help from her erstwhile protégée seemed farfetched. Leila's sudden turnabout concerning Waldo mystified Morgan, and she could only conclude that she didn't know as much about human nature as she had thought.

A commotion at the front entrance recalled Morgan's attention, and she and Annalee moved with the crowd to gape at the late arrivals—Jarvis O'Connell and a representative of the Suki.

The half-naked mottled creature crouched in the doorway, bringing with it a whiff of the swamps. Jarvis urged it to enter, and a space magically cleared.

General Cross and Miranda and the two Cetians hurried over. "We ah honored," Miranda said to Jarvis. "Please tell him that. And find out what he'd lak to drink." She managed not to look at the Suka.

Jarvis translated, and the Suka straightened to the full height of a female. A pregnant one, Morgan guessed, seeing the mound of stomach. The face was flat and still.

The Suka croaked, and the humans moved a pace backward. "She'll have beer," Jarvis said.

"I'll get it," Miranda offered, but the general held her by the arm while he signaled to one of his men.

"One beer and four brandies," he ordered, and while they waited Jarvis made introductions. The Suka's name was unpronounceable in Terran, he said, but her title was Best Mother. By virtue of her fecundity she was speaking for all the swamp dwellers.

Best Mother twitched a single fold of skin

above her left eye and uttered a long croaking
speech. "She is gratified that humans have
reached an accord," Jarvis said. "The Suki are
distressed when there is disharmony. So distressed that they were tempted to withhold all
their new harvest of firmax."

Both the general and the tall Cetian started to
speak, but Jarvis held up his hand. "She likes
the new treaty and is satisfied as long as no
more humans come to disturb the swamps."

An orderly came with a tray of drinks and
distributed them to Best Mother, General Cross,
Miranda, and the two Cetians. Jarvis stood
empty-handed in the circle, a flush rising from
his collar. "To the treaty," the general said, raising his glass ceremoniously.

"To the treaty." The others followed suit, all
except the Suka, who drained hers in great noisy
slurps. Jarvis, ignored, stared at a spot on the
far wall.

After an awkward silence the general cleared
his throat. "Uh, would she like something to
eat?" he asked Jarvis. "Perhaps you could, er,
guide her around the room."

Jarvis remained stiffly impassive.

"What's wrong with you, O'Connell?" the general snapped. "Find out what we're supposed
to do now. What do you think we pay you for,
anyway?"

Color suffused Jarvis's face as he conversed
with the Suka. It was a long conversation, but
the xenologist only reported tersely to the general that Best Mother was satisfied, that she
thanked them all and would return now to her
home.

Jarvis and Best Mother left, and the party
slowly returned to life. Morgan, however, was
too confused by a disturbing new thought to
want to socialize. She escaped to the kitchen.

Jarvis's reaction to the general's snub reminded her of other occasions when the testy little redhead had complained of military mentalities. She had often commiserated with him, agreeing that without his translating skills the base could not even operate, yet he had received no appreciation in the way of the status he so valued.

For the first time she wondered if she had been too hasty in placing all of her suspicions on Waldo. Too swayed by her own resentments. Jarvis began to emerge as an equally likely candidate: the only one who could talk to the Suki, who could bargain with them and report his own version to the general, who could manipulate both Terrans and Cetians to suit his special purposes or those of the Suki. Could he be out to amass a private fortune in firmax? Working for the Suki, to get rid of both camps of humans?

He had been a friend of Drake's, too, and had often visited the tower. And he had been *very* thick with Grikkoor, establishing an immediate rapport that in retrospect seemed unlikely for the reticent Suki.

Morgan returned to the party, where Miranda's guests were nibbling on yeastcake chicken legs and talking up a storm over the throbbing wail of a luroharp duet. She spotted Arnie dancing with their hostess. He saw Morgan and signaled behind his partner's back.

Morgan came to his rescue. "I'm sorry," she said, interrupting the couple. "I'm leaving now. Thanks for inviting me."

"Ah didn't." Miranda's smile was sugary.

"I'll see you home," Arnie said.

"But . . ." Miranda's protest, the music, and the chatter were all stilled as an armed squad of Cetians burst through the doorway.

"Back. Stand back, everyone." Arnie made a sign to his own men, who moved out of the crowd to station themselves strategically about the room. He confronted the Cetians. "Suppose you explain what this is all about."

The Cetians waved scatterguns and shouted. Morgan, though reasonably fluent in the Terran-derived language, caught only a few words: "Urroks. Axes. Over the walls. Dead. Treacherous scum." The shouts became an untranslatable storm of abuse.

The two Cetian ambassadors strode forward to confer with the soldiers. After a minute the tall one turned angrily to Arnie, all pretense of civility abandoned. "Where is your general?" he demanded.

General Cross took a position slightly behind Arnie. Morgan saw the hands of Arnie's men move within their clothing, and the bulges of pulse weapons appeared. "What is going on?" the general said with icy dignity. "You must realize that threatening us in this manner is already a violation of the treaty."

The Cetian snorted. "How dare you speak of the treaty, when even while prating of peace you were inciting the urroks to attack us. They killed two men and a child before we drove them off. Let the Suki judge who have broken the treaty; we will demand that all Terrans leave the planet immediately."

"Ridiculous!" The general stood his ground. "How could we incite the urroks when no one but the Suki can approach them? They seem to have become violent for some reason—one of our own people was attacked earlier this week—but neither we nor the Suki can account for it. You are welcome to take the case to them, however. In fact, we urge you to. After a display like this, you may well be the ones who will have to leave."

The two leaders glowered at one another. The Cetian finally spoke to his men, who lowered

their weapons. They left together, gold robes
and soldiers, stalking out in stiff anger.

Morgan let out her breath.

"Is this your doing, too?" Miranda hissed from
behind her. "Ah hope you sleep well tonight!"

Morgan started to answer, but stopped when
she saw the venomous tears of jealousy in Miranda's eyes. The woman was beyond reason,
she knew, understanding finally why the general's mind had been so poisoned against an innocuous teacher.

The party broke up. Arnie was already in conference with the general and his staff, and Morgan left alone.

The building that housed the bachelor civilians was quiet and dark. Morgan passed Jarvis's
quarters, and on an impulse tried the door. It
was unlocked, and she buried her scruples and
entered.

Her hand beamer revealed a studio room of
uncommon neatness: the bed unwrinkled, the
clothes hanging with precision in the open closet,
the desktop immaculate. She searched quickly
through the desk drawers, not exactly sure what
she was looking for. Any unusual correspondence,
memos, instructions, or receipts. Anything linking Jarvis to the Cetians or the Suki.

She found nothing but personal accretia and
the expected files and charts and annotated data
of a practicing xenologist. Almost relieved, she
shone the light for a final look around when
something white, out of place on the closet floor,
caught her eye.

It was one of the cotton gloves that Jarvis
always wore outside. This one was badly stained,
and as Morgan sniffed at it she detected the
unmistakable pungency of raw firmax.

She took the glove with her when she left the
room. It could be perfectly innocent, she told
herself. During the last day's negotiations the

xenologist must have gone often to the swamps in his role of interpreter.

The Suki, though, guarded the firmax paddies jealously. Why had Jarvis been allowed entry?

In her own room Morgan changed into coveralls, too keyed up to try to sleep. She could see Arnie's office from her window, and as soon as his light went on she hurried over.

Someone had arrived before her, however. Morgan stopped outside the door when she heard the voices.

"I hope you don't mind my waiting for you here. I just had to talk to someone." It was Miranda Cross, sounding curiously intimate with only a trace of her magnolia accent.

"No, of course not, but ... it's awfully late. Won't the general be looking for you?"

Morgan took her hand from the doorknob. She started to leave, but her feet stubbornly refused to carry her. She turned back.

"If he is, it won't hurt him to wonder. Lord knows I've waited for him often enough." Through the window Morgan caught a glimpse of Miranda in her party finery before a slender hand pulled down the shade.

The voice went on, increasingly querulous: "Arnie, you have no idea how it feels to be excluded every time something important is going on. I try so hard—you know that I do—but still I'm always on the outside. A decoration, that's all I am. Like tonight. Sure I can organize a party at the last minute, and sure, I'm fine to show off to his buddies here, and to Cetians, and even to that swamp creature, but when anything top-level comes up—who was at that meeting, anyway? I bet there were other women there—Annalee and that fat ox Dr. Oosten. But not the general's *wife*, you can be sure she wasn't invited, she's nobody, she's nothing but a pretty face and an empty head."

A sob caught in the voice, and after a protracted silence that made Morgan squirm Arnie answered softly. "I know how you feel."

Morgan stiffened. She covered her ears, but again could not force herself to leave.

When she listened again, her cheeks burned. "She's let me know, in subtle ways, that I'm not quite up to her intellectual standards. I'm not an Academy man, you know. Worked my way up through the ranks. Hell, I've never read those dusty old bookspools of hers and I wouldn't know a sonnet from a sonata."

Miranda murmured something that Morgan could not hear.

"No, it's important to her," Arnie said. "I sometimes feel that I'd do *anything* to pull myself up into a position where she'd *have* to respect me."

Morgan could not bear to hear any more. She stumbled away from the window, trying to blank out the overheard conversation. It persisted, however, replaying itself and shaming her with the realization of how insufferably patronizing she must have been.

I'd do anything. The words came back to torture her. How far had she driven him?

She dared not pursue the thought. Instead she remembered Arnie risking his life at the tower. She saw him again as he had faced the Cetians barely an hour ago. The threat in his eyes that had made them back down.

How could she doubt him? The strain was making her lose all perspective. If Arnie was disloyal, nothing in her world would be secure.

She had even considered marrying him. Not that he had spoken of it, but he was due for an Earthside post after this assignment, and she thought she knew what was on his mind.

It was on hers, too. Though she had been orphaned at nine and had grown up in government dorms, her warmest memories, as well as

her best adult fantasies, had always been of a
nuclear family. Arnie looked so much like the
husband-father figure of her imaginings that she
had felt a shock of recognition the first time she
had seen him.

The signals she had sent him, however, must
have been quite different. He had never opened
himself to her as he had to Miranda. But then—
the persistent voice would not be stilled—*how
well did she know him?*

She couldn't face either Arnie or Miranda.
Morgan walked quickly around the end of the
hut and collided in the darkness with another
hurrying figure.

"Leila! What are you doing out here?" she
whispered. The girl struggled to get away while
Morgan held her arm.

"Just walking. I ... couldn't sleep, and ...
please, let go of me. I'm not asking you what
your business is!"

Morgan released her, and Leila sped off in the
direction of the warehouse buildings adjoining
the rear stockade. Morgan followed, welcoming
the distraction. At least she could settle one
thing for sure—if Waldo was the lover Leila was
meeting.

Leila circled the testing lab and the ware-
houses, heading for the rear loading gate. It was
opened only when there were shipments, at other
times remaining stoutly secured but unguarded
except for the perimeter patrols. She removed
loose soil and slipped easily under, and after
allowing her a safe lead Morgan followed.

Outside the stockade wall she spied the shadowy figure racing through the clearing toward
the trees. The nearest patrol was just coming
into sight, and Morgan dropped to the grass
until he passed, then sprinted across.

She was too late; Leila was swallowed up by
the forest.

Morgan searched futilely for tracks, then sat on a stump while she pondered what to do next. If Leila wasn't meeting Waldo—and there would be no need for them to rendezvous outside the compound—the only alternative was so much worse that her mind balked.

A light glimmered toward the northeast, and Morgan set out after it, threading between the trees until her uneasy suspicions became a certainty: they were heading directly toward the Cetian base.

It was crazy to be in the woods at night, weaponless. Morgan thought of nocturnal crawlers and wild urroks and trigger-happy Cetian patrols. But she also thought of her disgrace and of Waldo running her classroom, and she continued after Leila.

She trailed the flickering light for an hour, lost it when she had to backtrack around an impassable thicket, sighted it again when the trees thinned. Nightflyers brushed her face and something ropy clung to her legs, but she pushed doggedly on.

Another hour passed, and the distance between Morgan and her quarry narrowed. Leila moved with increasing caution as they neared the Cetian end of the forest, and by the time she left the shelter of the trees Morgan was close behind her.

Morgan remained hidden, watching. A wide marshy area formed a natural moat before the log-walled camp, and Leila seemed to be searching for an access route. She had turned off her light and made several false starts, stepping into the ooze, before she switched on her low beam and located a lane of solid footing.

Morgan pointed her own beamer at the ground and followed quietly. Leila was halfway across the marsh and Morgan a hundred feet behind her when they were both caught in a glaring spotlight. Morgan turned and ran blindly, plunging to one hip in the mire. Just as she pulled herself out, a warning scatterblast inches from her head stopped any further flight.

A glowering guard marched both women through the gate. He prodded Morgan with his gunbarrel and shouted something in a low Cetian dialect, but she was too rattled to understand.

Another guard came and grilled them in Terran. "Your business? What is your business?" He too waved a scattergun.

Leila, her face ashen in the gloom, turned from Morgan to the two men and moaned softly.

Morgan said nothing, either. She was in it now, she thought. Her finger-needle was empty, and she doubted that Leila had a weapon. But even if she did, Morgan no longer knew what to think about the girl and her motives.

The guards conferred. They searched both Morgan and Leila, relieved them of their beamers and a small mirror of Leila's, and pushed them into a narrow room within the wall. A bolt slid shut and they were alone in the darkness.

Leila continued to cry.

"All right, that isn't going to help," Morgan said. "Suppose you tell me what this is all about."

Receiving no response, she pressed. "Who is it you were coming to meet? Where is he?" Then, more gently: "I'd like to understand."

Leila swallowed her sobs. "His name is Balim, and he isn't at all like everyone says about the Cetians."

She stopped, and Morgan could imagine her defiant expression. "Go on," she said softly.

Leila blew her nose. "He's gentle and he doesn't care the least bit about their wars. He only wants us to get along peacefully—just like we talked about in class—and he said if I helped him we could make it happen, at least on this planet."

"Help him—how?"

Leila didn't answer for a long moment. "I told him about the extra troops we had, disguised as civilians. And about the tower and all the guns there. I found out where they were and told him.

"I didn't know Drake would be killed," she wailed. "Balim said that if the Suki found out about the tower and the soldiers there would have to be a new treaty and all this hatred and distrust would come to an end.

"I didn't know that you'd get the blame, either. But I couldn't tell the truth yet, because Balim and I . . ." She stopped again.

"You want to be together," Morgan prompted.

"You *do* understand! He said that after a few months when both our people had gotten to be on better terms we could meet openly and no one would mind. Not even Mother."

"So that's why you were pretending with Waldo."

"Mother knew I was meeting someone, and I couldn't have her guessing the truth—not yet.

"It almost worked, too." The young voice gained strength. "You saw, at the party. The new treaty was just what we wanted. Everything out in the open. No more hoarding arms and expecting an invasion every day. If only those urroks . . ." The despair was back. "Now everything's just as bad, or worse. I went to the woods to find Balim, to ask him what we should do now. But he wasn't at the meeting place, so I thought maybe I'd find him at the wall, that he might be on duty and couldn't get away."

"Why didn't you ask for him, then? I should think he'd help *you*, at least."

"I . . . I was afraid. He said never to come here."

"But surely . . . you've been a spy for them,

for God's sake. Don't you think they'd be grate-
ful?"

She began to sob again. "I don't know. Nothing
is like I expected. He said if we were ever caught
we should pretend not to know each other. I
don't know what to do now!"

Morgan comforted her as best she could. "Let's
see what they decide to do with us. If they think
we're spies, you may *have* to appeal to Balim.
But try to stay calm." She embraced the trembling girl, far from calm herself but trying to hide
it. She couldn't help remembering what she had
heard about the Cetians and their cruelty to
prisoners.

It was dawn when they were released from
the room and pushed toward an airsled waiting
in the open courtyard. "Where are you taking
us?" Morgan demanded."

She received no answer, and repeated her question in low Cetian.

"You'll see," grunted the pilot. The guards
bound Morgan's arms and legs and tossed her
into the cargo hold. Leila followed, almost on
top of her.

"Wait, wait. You must tell Balim!" Leila
shouted, but the door snapped shut on her
words."

"Don't worry, they're probably going to dump
us outside our own gate, as some sort of a warning," Morgan said. "From what I've heard, we're
lucky to still have all of our fingers and toes—
not to mention worse."

"Balim says that talk is all lies," Leila said.

The airsled rose with a sharp bounce and the
two women rolled apart. "Not much of a pilot,
is he?" Morgan observed. She twisted to a sitting position and strained to see through the
rear vent. They seemed to be going north, away
from the Terran camp, but she did not mention
it to Leila.

"What are you going to tell them about me?" Leila's voice quavered. "I don't suppose you could . . . make up some story. Until all this blows over."

"I may not have a chance to tell anyone anything," Morgan said quietly. "Either of us." The airsled was angling for descent, directly over the plateau of the urroks.

Morgan revised her estimate of the pilot. In a difficult maneuver the airsled dropped, banked steeply, and hung. The cargo door sprang open and the two prisoners tumbled six feet to the ground.

Morgan landed on her back, her wind knocked out. She recovered to find Leila sprawled motionless a short distance away. Her head had hit a rock, and at first glance she looked dead. Morgan wriggled over and found a pulse. She tried to arrange the inert form more comfortably, but she could do little with her bound hands.

She began to work at the ropes. There was some give, but not enough. She found a rock with a sharp edge, and by alternately chewing on the rope fibers and sawing them on the rock she cut through enough strands to loosen her hands. She quickly untied her feet, then did the same for the unconscious girl. A quick glance around the plateau had inspired her with the need for haste: the rocky cliff that bordered it on one side was studded with dark holes that could only be the caves of the urroks.

Leila stirred and Morgan helped her up; there was no time to wait on injuries. "We've got to get out of here," she said, half-dragging the limp figure.

The morning rays of Hedron slanted into the caves, and Morgan saw movement. A brown shape, ursinoid but walking upright, stood in one of the openings. It reached long arms toward a pile of some unidentifiable foodstuff, saw the two humans, and froze.

Leila came to consciousness with a gasp. Morgan continued to support her as they circled in front of the caves, crouching behind boulders whenever possible but exposed much of the time to the view of the rapidly gathering urroks.

The creatures packed the cave mouths. They growled and milled, but made no move to come out. The women passed by safely.

The flat portion of the plateau gave way to a rocky labyrinth of ravines and gullies, but there were no more caves. Morgan chose a route down a canyon that looked passable. Leila walked without support, and Morgan was just beginning to breathe easily when they rounded a turn and came face to face with a pack of a dozen or so urroks.

Leila screamed and turned to run. Morgan grabbed her arm and stopped her when she saw that the beasts did not appear to notice them. Most of the urroks were unarmed, but a few still clutched in their claws wooden handles from which the blades had been removed.

The creatures moved sluggishly, their heads hanging and their eyes, whenever they looked up, blank and film-covered. A frothy drool dripped from their muzzles.

Morgan and Leila flattened themselves against the ravine wall until the last urrok had shuffled past. Leila fanned the air. "I didn't know they stank so!"

"I don't think they usually do," Morgan said. "These seem to have been drugged. I wouldn't be surprised if they're the same ones that attacked the Cetians."

"Could be. They're coming from that direction, and as slow as they're moving it would have taken them all night to get this far."

Leila sounded alert, and her color was better. "How does your head feel?" Morgan asked.

Leila fingered the lump behind her ear and winced. "Not too bad. At least, I'll be okay once we get out of here. What happened, anyway? Why were we dumped like that?"

"Can't you guess? We were obviously intended to be victims of the urroks. 'A tooth for a tooth' punishment in exchange for the Cetians who were killed. It's their justice."

Leila's eyes were wide. "I can't believe . . . but . . . anyway, I'm sure Balim didn't know about it."

"Perhaps not." Morgan left her that crumb. "They must have expected the urroks to be as warlike as they were last night. If they'd known . . . I can't figure out what's been happening to those creatures."

"You said drugged. We wouldn't have done it, would we?"

"As far as I know, we don't even know how. But I'm going to find out as soon as I can from Jarvis what the Suki have been up to."

"If we ever get home. Where is this leading us, anyway?" Leila looked up at the rock walls of the canyon, and ahead where it seemed to twist endlessly into more barren terrain.

"We should be out of this soon." Morgan sighted from the sun. "Unfortunately, we'll probably come out somewhere in back of the Cetian base. But we can take to the swamps; we should be safe with the Suki."

Morgan's guess proved correct. They skirted the Cetian clearing by way of the marshes, sticking close to the edge where the footing was fairly safe. When the reeds thinned and they were forced by their exposure to the Cetians to go deeper, the swamp became too treacherous. They stopped at a clump of knob-rooted *supsa* trees, and Morgan rigged a sun reflector from

Leila's belt buckle. She was counting on a quick response from the jealously territorial Suki.

One came in minutes, its face folded and its croak raspingly urgent. It indicated in clear motions that they were to leave the swamp immediately for the Cetian clearing.

Morgan tried to pantomime that they were not Cetians and that they must cross the swamp to get home.

The Suki left, and returned with reinforcements. Together they tried to force the women back toward the edge of the swamp.

Morgan thought of the only Suka who might help them. "Grikkoor," she croaked, as best she could. If she could only make them understand. "Grik-koor," she repeated, trying to utilize Jarvis's half-forgotten language instructions.

One Suka rippled a skinflap. It spoke to its companions and they all melted into the reeds.

Morgan and Leila settled themselves on the dry island of the *supsa* roots. Leila fell into a doze, and Morgan worried about concussion. After a long hour Grikkoor appeared, accompanied by Jarvis O'Connell.

"I couldn't believe it," the xenologist exclaimed, staring at the mud-covered women. He fixed on Morgan. "From the description, I thought it must be you. But after all that's happened..." He shook his helmeted head. "And coming from the Cetian camp. I felt sorry for you before, but it looks now as though the general was right."

Leila opened her eyes. "No, it was me; I'm the spy." She closed them again.

"Oh, believe what you like," Morgan said. "Leila may be hurt, and we're both dead on our feet. Just get us home if you can." She glanced sharply from Jarvis to Grikkoor. "That is, if you and your friend can spare the time from making axes and feeding the urroks whatever it is that sets them off on their rampages."

"Ohmygod." Jarvis's freckles stood out sharply as he paled. "How did you know about that?"

"It was just a guess, until now. But why? Are you trying to corner the firmax market for yourself? Get rid of all the rest of us?" Even as she said the words, watching Jarvis in his consternation, Morgan couldn't bring herself to believe them.

"Ohmygod," he repeated, twisting his gloved hands. "You can't think that! You wouldn't tell anyone that, would you? I had nothing to do with it. In fact, I only found out last night, after I came here with Best Mother after the reception."

"Why don't you tell us on the way back?" Morgan was still uneasy about Leila. She considered waiting with her while Jarvis went for an airsled, but she didn't trust him and she wasn't sure it would even be possible to land.

Grikkoor led them on the narrow trails of solid ground. Leila walked behind him, steady enough, followed by Morgan and then Jarvis.

The xenologist needed no urging to unburden himself. "I had no idea of the control the Suki have over the urroks," he said. "Best Mother told me a lot of surprising things when she decided to trust me.

"It's the breakthrough I've been hoping for." He didn't disguise the ringing note of pride.

"Yes, congratulations," Morgan said. They were crossing an unstable bit of bog, and she dared not raise her eyes from the trail. "But go on, please."

Jarvis continued. "The Suki drugged the urroks' food with a firmax derivative that makes them wild, provided them with weapons, and pointed them at a target. The ones you ran into the other day, and stopped, were heading for our camp."

"Grikkoor was leading them?"

"No, following them. After they'd thrown a few axes at the stockade and the drug had worn off, he intended to herd them back to their plateau. The effect only lasts a couple of hours, and then they become confused and dopey."

"Yes, we ran into the ones that had attacked the Cetians. Harmless as babies. But why are the Suki doing all this? What's their angle?"

"You had it right, except for my part. To get rid of all us humans. The Suki have never liked our being here, neither us nor the Cetians. They originally agreed on two small camps, remember? Just to receive the firmax and give them the metals they want. But the way we've both been expanding and arming and bringing in more and more troops—they don't want their swamps turned into a battleground."

"But why the urroks? The Suki know their rights under the Charter. Couldn't they just ask us to leave? Withhold the firmax?"

"They made a contract, and they don't go back on their word. They hoped we'd be frightened and all leave voluntarily."

They were out of the bog, and the trail widened. As Morgan relaxed she recalled her previous trip through the swamp. "Then it was the Suki, too, who moved the markers that time I got lost?"

Leila turned her head. "No, it was Balim. He did it the first time we met in the forest, so no one would come on us from the tower. But"—her face twisted with misery—"he said he'd move them back right away. I thought he'd done it."

Morgan felt for Leila in her disillusionment, but there was nothing she could say. They all faced a more serious problem. "What will the Suki do now? They must know that we can't give up the firmax."

"I've been talking to Best Mother all night, trying to come up with an acceptable compro-

mise. She's finally agreed to a plan that I'm
sure will give the general apoplexy, but I can't
see that there's any other choice."

"And that is?"

Jarvis hesitated. "Well, I guess you'll know
soon enough. The Suki want all humans off the
planet except for one of us and one Cetian. They'll
keep supplying firmax at the same trade rate
and they'll allow regular landings for pickup,
but we have to train them to maintain the signal tower and the landing field. They want to be
totally in control from now on."

"And what about you? Will you be the Terran
to remain?" Tough duty, Morgan thought. She
turned to watch Jarvis's reaction.

He flushed. "Actually, you were their first
choice. Was I out of line when I told them you
wouldn't be interested?"

"Good Lord, no!"

"That's what I thought. Anyway, they'll accept me, even though I'm no supermom."

He considered it an honor, she realized. And
maybe it was. The neophyte had pulled the fat
out of the fire for all of them, and if it was his
idea of a reward to be marooned with Suki . . .

She herself couldn't get away from Hedron II
fast enough. The only thing that troubled her
was leaving unfinished whatever existed between
her and Arnie. That is, if there had ever really
been anything. She still smarted when she recalled his conversation with Miranda, but in
spite of it—or perhaps because of it—she knew
that she had to see him.

When they arrived at the compound and Leila,
Jarvis, and Grikkoor were closeted with the general, Morgan cleaned up and went directly to
the security office.

Arnie seemed to be expecting her, dressed in
fresh fatigues and smelling of aftershave. Though
initially he was angry—"What was I supposed

to think? Annalee's been frantic and the general's ready to bust me for letting you get out"—he calmed when he heard her explanation.

"So it looks like we'll all be leaving," she finished.

Arnie shuffled papers on his desk. His brow was still knotted. "Morgan, I apologize. I didn't want to doubt you, but with everything that's been happening. . . ."

"It's all right. I know how bad it looked."

He squared himself with sudden resolution. "Don't take another assignment."

She held her breath.

"Maybe this isn't the right moment, but it's been on my mind for some time. You and me, I mean. Do you think we could make it as a team?"

He took her hands and spoke of Earth and of a shared home for the two of them. It was her fantasy materialized. Arnie fit it perfectly, just as she had always thought he would. His words, too, were the ones she had hoped to hear—her own scenario, rehearsed so often she should not have had to fumble for a response.

Unaccountably, however, she did. According to the script she should have been floating on a cloud, but her feet were still firmly anchored to the plank floor of Arnie's office. Instead of a cozy Earthside nest she thought of worlds she had not yet seen—the diamond mountains of Midia, the firepools of Beta Hydri I, the colored snows of Jaspre. Stalwart colony children and alien younglings who flew.

Arnie waited, and she knew what she must tell him. She would have cried a little, except for the sight of Miranda approaching from the mess with a covered coffee tray. Arnie would be well comforted.

*   *   *

"*The general must have written you a good letter, then,*" Billingsgate said. "*I see you got posted to Midia.*"

"*I don't think so. The letter, I mean. Oh, he probably rated me as 'satisfactory'—the least he could say—but he wouldn't have given me any raves. He still didn't like me much.*

"*My assignment to Midia was pure luck. I'd been on a couple of routine assignments—you have them there—and I was suffering from burnout. I'd been approved for an Earth leave when a vacancy turned up on Midia, and I was available. I guess Corps Central figured it was just what I needed.*"

IV. The Towers of Trianka
1

The planet Midia sparkled on the viewscreen, a jade-green pendant frosted with streamers of cirrus. Magnified, surface features appeared: the deep blue of water, the arching black spine of a mountain, and finally, as they turned, the soaring glassy towers of the fabled capital, Trianka.

The magnification disappeared and Midia hung again like a showcased jewel. Morgan loosened her grip on her armrests and let out her breath, a sigh that was echoed throughout the rows of passengers.

"I can't believe we're really here—and that it's as beautiful as I've heard all my life." Morgan's seatmate, Elli Trask, continued to gaze wide-eyed at the screen. "I'll admit now, I've been afraid of being disappointed." A nervous giggle escaped her. "I don't know what I would have done."

You poor child; we're not there yet, Morgan thought. She knew what Midia meant to Elli. The young woman had attached herself to Morgan at Cygni Station, and during the month of forced proximity in the commercial hypership *Outreach* had regaled the teacher with what must have been every bleak detail of her nineteen years on the colony world Centauri Ceres.

"You know what this trip costs," Elli said. She played with an end of her long braid of brown hair. "I've spent almost my whole bundle."

"Yes, it's one-way for you, isn't it?" Morgan turned from the screen to study her companion. Elli had dressed for the landing in one of her newly purchased outfits, a spangled tunic and wide-legged electric-blue trousers that ill became her squat heavy-world figure. Her plain face was animated now and almost pretty with the look of wonder inspired by the image on the screen.

Morgan breathed a prayer that Elli's hopes would be fulfilled. On the death of her father the farmgirl had sold the land she had inherited and invested the entire sum in a dream. Trianka, the pleasure city. As far removed from the dusty plains of Ceres as five thousand credits could ensure, and with no way to return.

Ah well, perhaps it would be all right, Morgan thought. The Midians were notably hospitable, imposed no restrictions on immigrants, and welcomed visitors with an enthusiasm that was famed even beyond the sector.

She herself had hardly believed her luck in being assigned here. After the recent succession of backwater planets on which she had served, Midia was a plum of a duty.

"A paid vacation, really," the Corps director on Cygni had told her. "The Medians want one Terran teacher in their schools, but you'll see— there'll be very little actual work for you to do.

"They want their children to be completely free from prejudice," he had explained in response to Morgan's raised eyebrows. "You and the other selected offworlders serve as model mentors when their young are most impressionable. They grow up to be . . . incredibly gracious. You'll see." The director had smiled dreamily.

"You've been there?" Morgan had asked.

"For the most ... memorable ... year of my life."

Morgan had heard similar reports. Trianka's reputation as an ultimate resort was hampered only by the difficulty of access from the Terran worlds—a double-jump run that few but the wealthy could afford. The *Outreach*'s staterooms had been occupied by rare-metal barons, interstellar bankers, retired diplomats, and dealers in gems. All except 301, Trask and Farraday, which had held a nervous teacher and a wildly expectant dirt farmer's daughter.

The passengers were all now in the shuttle preparing for descent. The image of Midia disappeared from the viewscreen, replaced by pictograph strap-in instructions. A steward stopped at Morgan's row, reclined the seats, and checked the bindings and aircushions. "Honey, you've gotta be in tighter than that," he said to Elli, crushing the expensive fabric of her trouser legs as he adjusted the harness.

"Medications?" offered a second attendant. "Something to calm you or put you out?"

Elli took a happy pill, but Morgan shook her head. She preferred to take the deceleration straight and arrive clearheaded. She closed her eyes and allowed her body to relax bone by bone into the yielding softness. Elli chattered on—nonsense, the tranquilizer already at work— but Morgan ignored her, trying to empty her mind. She had chosen no mantra for the descent, trusting one to come to her, and when it didn't she surrendered herself to an image that had been hovering for some time at the edge of consciousness. It was a diamond, the symbol of wealth, the symbol of Midia: many-faceted, gleaming with light, perfect in its cold beauty. The galaxy's continued greed for the rare stone was, Morgan knew, the foundation of Midia's economy, the basis for the luxurious life-style of its inhabitants. The black mountain that she had glimpsed in the viewscreen was veined with diamond deposits unequaled in the known worlds.

Morgan rode with the gleaming stone to a feather-soft landing, unbuckling from her couch with almost no twinges.

Elli was gray-faced. "My clothes," she wailed, surveying her hopelessly wrinkled and sweat-stained finery.

"Never mind—you'll have to strip and change anyway for decontamination," Morgan said.

Elli's mouth gaped.

"It's not so bad," Morgan reassured her. "I'll go through with you."

Morgan spoke truer than she had thought— the Triankans had refined the usually unpleasant procedure to a warm and perfumed series of infra-baths. Except for the long lines and the waiting, the two women passed the hour with no discomfort. They emerged from the last chamber dressed in soft white one-piece garments and flexible sandals.

A Midian attendant came to guide them through the registration process, again streamlined to painlessness. Morgan presented her disk and slender fingers flew over keyboards. In minutes she was ushered into the reception area.

A series of rooms that resembled open courtyards admitted the sky through glassy walls. Smiling Midians placed garlands of tissue-thin petals on Morgan's head and shoulders. Others offered fruit and sparkling drinks, and led her to a cushioned seat beside a stream that ran over jewel-toned rocks. "Rest and refresh yourself, Morgan Farraday," her guide said in perfect though stiffly stylized Terran. "Oo-lors has been apprised of your arrival, and will be here soon."

Elli, standing in the doorway, exclaimed in

pleasure. Soft-footed guides led her, her face radiant, off in another direction.

Morgan sipped her drink, which tasted faintly of apricots and almonds, and studied her hosts with the unabashed interest of a first visitor. She had heard so much: the "sweet-eyed Midians" of the poets, the "gentle sylphs," the "most loving children of the stars."

They appeared to be all that. The men were tall and slender and pale, with silvery hair that fell like clouds to their shoulders. The women were more willowy still, with waists that a child's hand's could span and the barest suggestion of breasts and hips. Both the men and women wore pastel garments of the same cut as Morgan's, cloth that contoured itself to their figures, free-flowing and easy. They moved lightly, with an effortless grace, and their eyes were indeed the stuff of poetry.

Someone touched Morgan's shoulder. "So how do we meet your appraisal?"

She started, and flushed, but the smiling face held no censure. "I am Oo-lors, your *aliti*. That is, your personal host and guide and it-is-to-be-hoped friend. I am sorry to be late, but as in all cities we in Trianka sometimes have problems with traffic. Have you been waiting long?"

"No, not long at all." Morgan moved slightly to allow Oo-lors to sit beside her. His warmly approving gaze allowed no doubt as to how she met *his* appraisal.

Morgan returned the smile, but reacted to the obvious admiration with a touch of skepticism. She knew how she looked, and how he would see her. She was thirty-nine years old, well past the first blush. Her body, spare and trim though it was, would appear thick to a Midian, and she had lived on enough frontier worlds to garner her share of wind and sun lines.

The Midian guide had a flawless complexion.

Still, Morgan estimated his age at something near her own. His well-defined features lacked the youthful softness of some of the other Midians, but it was mostly his manner—serene and confident—that bespoke maturity. His deep-set eyes continued to regard her steadily.

Midian eyes. They were large and slightly slanted, and set wider apart than the human norm. Oo-lors's seemed to glisten with an overlay of some aqueous substance, so that it was difficult to accurately define their color or even the exact configuration of the irises. They were truly what romantics had described as "melting," for as she looked into them Morgan felt something dissolve in her, something hard that she knew was better lost.

She turned away in confusion.

"We *will* be friends," Oo-lors said, touching her lightly on the hand.

"Are you Midians telepathic, too?" She felt a vague sense of invasion.

"No, but we are sensitive to . . . auras. Do you know what I mean?"

"Of course I do, though I've never been sure I believed in that sort of thing."

"Yet you practice meditation."

"It has its uses. But how do you know so much about me?"

"I read your profile."

He winced at her sudden start. "Please, do not be alarmed. It is only to know how I can make your stay here more pleasant."

A green-gowned nymph drifted by with a tray of succulent meats. Diamonds glittered in her hair. Oo-lors speared a seafood morsel and offered it to Morgan. His ingenuous smile disarmed her. "So what did you find out about me?" she asked.

"That you have a practical nature, and because you are somewhat puritanical—by our standards, at least—you may look with disfavor upon the more hedonistic aspects of our lives. I must persuade you not to judge us too harshly."

She was ready with a defensive retort when she realized that he was teasing. A relief. She had never considered herself puritanical. In fact, she had sometimes worried about the opposite extreme, a mature single spacefarer with no ties. She couldn't help wondering what Oo-lors's standards were.

His first statement about her character, however, was on the mark. "I *did* come here to work," she said. "Are you connected with the school?" Such concerns seemed out of place in the sybaritic atmosphere of the room, but she was curious, and Oo-lors, she was sure, would never broach the topic.

A group of strolling musicians playing lutelike instruments paused before the portly Cetian and his *aliti* on the other side of the stream. The soft notes of the serenade blended with the gently lapping water.

"You are not to think about such things now," Oo-lors said. "You must relax and take time to acclimate yourself. All the time you need." He leaned toward her, a slight frown disturbing the smoothness of his brow. "But I am being remiss. I can sense that you grow impatient with our reception salon. Perhaps you would like to see something of the city before you settle yourself in your quarters?" He rose in a fluid movement and made her a slight bow. "I am at your disposal."

"Yes, I *would* like to see where I'm to stay. But my luggage . . ."

"It has already been through the sterilizers and been sent ahead."

"My money—I have to change my vouchers."

"They are in the computers. We carry no currency here."

"Well, then . . ." She sprang to her feet with a small bounce; no grace at all. The small-planet gravity would take some getting used to, she thought. As would having her needs met before she even voiced them. Oo-lors offered his arm, and with his light guidance she tried to approximate the gliding walk of the Midians.

"No, I am not connected with the school," Oo-lors said. "The *aliti* is a profession peculiar to Midia. Perhaps you will appreciate it someday, if you do not now."

"Of course I appreciate you," she insisted. "I've never had such a lovely welcome." She wondered if Elli was faring as well, and looked around for her as they passed through the rooms filled with *Outreach* passengers and their attentive hosts.

Morgan spotted the girl from Ceres in a secluded corner, deep in conversation with a Midian youth of extraordinary beauty. She considered going over, but changed her mind.

"Your friend is in good hands," Oo-lors said. "You can contact her at any time."

"How can I find out where she's staying?"

"You have a vocom in your quarters. The *Outreach* passengers are all entered."

"Yes. Of course." Morgan felt as gauche an outworlder as Elli. She continued to marvel as they left the spaceport by a room-sized underground transport that moved with no sound or sense of motion.

They exited in the city proper.

The towers rose like fragile stalks, skyscrapers two thousand feet high that appeared as transparent and light as the sky itself. Between them stretched acres of green parks and wide lanes where ground traffic flowed as smoothly and silently as Procyon honey. Slender Midians and offworlders in a variety of human figure types strolled the footpaths or rode the slideways. In the crowds Morgan noticed a dozen or so human-oid aliens as well as a sprinkling of the more exotic oxygen-breathers. No one, she thought, could judge the Midians xenophobic.

"Your apartment is in the Amasit," Oo-lors said, indicating the nearest tower. They walked along a path shaded by broad-leafed trees, on stones that exuded a fragrance. The pedestrian thoroughfare was busy, but dividing hedges gave an illusion of privacy. Morgan caught snatches of conversation in a variety of tongues from neighboring paths.

They arrived at the Amasit tower, which on its lower levels housed a shopping district that in itself was a small city. Oo-lors guided Morgan through a few of the glittering arcades, past shops displaying stunning art and luxurious clothing and diamonds to reel the senses. Pear-shaped teardrops vied with walnut-sized mar-quises, adamantine fire unadorned and set in finished jewelry to tempt the most varied tastes.

Wherever they went, they were treated with courtesy. Every Midian smiled. The prices Morgan saw were staggering, but the shops were full. Cetians and Elyrians and Terrans looked and compared and calculated, whispered with their companions, looked some more, and finally, inevitably, bought.

"Do you feel the urge?" Oo-lors asked.

"On my salary?" Morgan grinned wryly.

"No one leaves Trianka without at least one diamond. But for you there is no hurry. When the time comes, I can find you better bargains than these."

"Your cousin, who just happens to be in the business?" Morgan said, laughing.

"Everyone has a cousin in the business," Oo-lors agreed, "but I spoke truthfully. I can help you."

The shade of reproach in his voice shamed

her. Why was she always looking for flaws? she thought. Too many years on raw planets had made her skeptical of smooth surfaces. She would have to watch herself or she would do the Corps no service.

She gave him her friendliest smile. "I'll remember it." She took his arm. "All of this richness is making me tired, though. I'd like to see my apartment now."

He reacted with quick concern. "I am so sorry. I had forgotten that our days are long by your standards. And our nights. It would be wise to rest now, so that you may enjoy our evening pleasures."

"A night on the town? I'm game, if I can hold up."

Oo-lors led her to a bank of elevators. The one he selected was furnished with couches and lifted them gently to the sixty-first floor.

In the reception lobby she looked through a wall into the sky and the deeper blue of the harbor. Beyond the farthest tower a passenger balloon drifted over the water.

Morgan had an outside apartment, four light and airy rooms equipped with conveniences the function of which she could only guess. Oo-lors showed her how to opaque the window wall, demonstrated the kitchen and bathroom and entertainment units, keyed her in to the vocom, and then tactfully withdrew, promising to meet her in four hours for the evening tour.

Morgan struggled with the bathtub dials until she gave up and asked the vocom for help. A Midian voice instructed her, in Terran, and soon she was relaxing in a foamy perfumed bath. She regarded the tips of her toes dreamily as she wondered what kindly quirk of fate had delivered her to this galactic haven.

Her bed was a cloud of softness that did everything including sing her to sleep. She napped

for two hours and awoke refreshed and raven-
ously hungry. She pulled on a robe and inspected
the kitchen again. The fresh-food units were well
stocked, but she decided against cooking, sus-
pecting that Oo-lors's excursion would include
dinner. She settled for coffee and a sandwich
from the autoserve to tide her over.

Munching the familiar processed gluten, she
thought about the coming entertainment. The
mere mention of the pleasure clubs of Trianka
had brought life to the eyes of the most jaded
Outreach passengers. Elli had talked of little
else, worrying about her clothes and her lack of
social skills, until Morgan had become slightly
infected herself.

She wouldn't want to show up poorly. Not in
front of Oo-lors, professional guide though he
might be.

She glanced at her watch. She would just
have time to zip down to the shops and pick up
something more appropriate to wear than the
rather utilitarian outfits that she had brought.

She spent more than she should have, but the
pale green sheath did wonders for her figure
and for her morale. She coiled her hair into a
low Psyche knot and circled it with the rope of
glowstones her students on Hedron had given
her. A touch of color to her cheeks and lips, and
she was ready.

She had a few minutes to spare, and called
Elli.

The visiplate presented a startling apparition.
"I've spent the whole afternoon shopping and at
the beauty parlour," Elli said. She pirouetted
before the plate. "What do you think?"

Elli's gown was of irridescent Lurian silk,
the bodice cut low on her ample bosom and the
skirt slit to reveal an expanse of heavy thigh.
Diamonds set in petals of ridium glittered in
her ears, and ridium combs adorned her hair.

The thick brown braid was gone, replaced by a bleached, cottony mass, frizzed and fluffed to imitate the Midians'. Instead of falling like a cloud, however, it stood out electrically from her head, giving her a permanently startled appearance.

Morgan didn't know what to say. Elli continued to preen, with an expression half embarrassed and half smug. She took Morgan's silence for approval and gave her dress a final twitch of adjustment. "I've never seen such beautiful things!" she enthused. "And this apartment—it's everything I dreamed of, back on Ceres."

Morgan caught glimpses of furnishings that made her own rooms seem Spartan. Elli's face glowed, and Morgan continued to hold her tongue. She knew about Elli's finances, but how could she puncture such happiness? Besides, she was too conscious of her own recent extravagance to be able to rebuke Elli. The new green dress suddenly seemed to mock her, and she moved out of Elli's range to put on a cloak.

"I haven't tried the kitchen yet, but it's all automatic," the breathless voice went on. "And oh yes, there's even a maid. My clothes were all pressed and hung up. And the bathtub—I couldn't believe it!"

She paused, and Morgan came back to the visiplate. Awkward or not, she knew that she had to look out for her young friend. Her own living expenses were being underwritten by the Midians, and they were far more modest than Elli's. She couldn't stand by and watch the girl squander her nest egg. "But—are you sure you can afford all that?" she ventured cautiously.

Elli laughed. "I knew you'd say that. It *is* expensive, but it's just for a week. Ai-won—he's my *aliti*—suggested I try it. He says I deserve the best. After that he says he'll help me find another place if I want to move.

"Morgan, he's the most ... I don't know how to say it even, except that I didn't think I'd ever meet anyone like him. And the most incredible part is—he feels the same way about me!"

"Are you telling me that you're in love?" It was a foolish question; Elli radiated her feelings.

"Please don't look so disapproving. I know it's too fast, but Ai-won says it often happens that way here. He says Trianka is a city meant for lovers."

"You know, of course, that being charming is part of his job. We all have our *alitis*."

"Of course I know it," Elli said crossly. "I knew too that you'd try to spoil things." She pouted. "It won't work, though. I know that Ai-won is sincere, so you can just save your breath."

Morgan backed off. "Those are lovely earrings," she said. "I looked at diamonds, too, but so far I've resisted."

Elli remained defensive. She fingered the earrings. "Ai-won knew someone who gave me a really good price." Unable to hold her pique, she began to bubble again. "We're going diving tomorrow, and then on a balloon tour. Tonight we're going to the Crystal Cave—it's the best club in Trianka."

And the priciest, I'll wager, Morgan thought.

"He's picking me up in a few minutes. I'm sorry I can't talk longer." Elli cut off the conversation and Morgan was left troubled.

What would happen to Elli when her funds ran out? The usual expedient, finding a job, wouldn't be so easy in Trianka, where all of the service positions seemed to be filled by Midians.

Far worse for Elli, though, would be Ai-won's defection. Morgan felt strongly that she should warn Elli again, but she knew it would be useless.

Elli had had so little joy in her life. Morgan

recalled the girl's account of her childhood, working like a field drone on a frontier station. A mother who had hanged herself. A father embittered by grief and loneliness. No other human contacts except for convict workers and an occasional trader.

No wonder she had listened in awe to the traders' accounts of Trianka and had made it her goal. If ever fairy tales came true, Morgan thought, it should happen for Elli.

Maybe it would, she told herself. Cold logic didn't have to always prevail. At any rate, she couldn't let imagined problems spoil her own evening. She suspected that the entertainment would be on her, and checked her credit balance with the vocom. Assured that it was okay, even with the new dress, she waited for Oo-lors with unclouded anticipation.

He arrived with flowers and chocolates.

Morgan giggled.

"I understood it was a custom of your world," he said, puzzled.

"I've been away a long time," she said. "Maybe such rituals have been revived." She received his offerings and soothed his vanity with a whistle of admiration for his evening attire. His clinging tunic was space-black and his moonbeam hair was caught in a net of stars.

Morgan thought of Elli and avoided looking too deeply into his eyes.

They dined at the top of an oceanside tower, watching the flares of the tide-riders. Afterward, they strolled the phosphorescent beach with hordes of other tourists and listened to the music from the lava caves.

"Which is the Crystal Cave?" Morgan asked.

He indicated the one with the flitterpad and the largest crowd in front. "There are others that are quieter. Or I can get us a private room if you wish to sample any of our more arcane pleasures."

"I've heard about them. Even to wire-heading. Is it true?"

He shrugged. "Anything can be purchased."

She sensed his unease. "Don't worry, I'm not about to scramble my brain. The Crystal Cave will do fine."

A moving ramp bore them downward, into a cavern that seemed to stretch endlessly into dimly lit underground recesses. The main area, at the entrance, was illuminated by glowing crystal patches on the rock walls. Tables ringed a dance floor, and a band played music with a beat that echoed polyphonically from the walls and ceiling.

Morgan located Elli almost immediately, her strident laughter cutting through the music and the din of voices. She occupied a clear space on the dance floor, drunkenly attempting to follow the steps of two Midian youths. They twirled her from one to the other until she finally collapsed against the handsomer one, her *aliti*. Morgan could not help but notice the glance the two young men exchanged as they half-carried Elli back to a corner banquette.

"Would you like to join your friend?" Oo-lors asked.

Morgan shook her head. She thought of how Elli's mother had died, and while she did not blame the girl for her excesses neither did she care to witness them. She chose a table near the entrance, and when next she looked back Elli and her companions were gone.

To one of the private inner rooms, she assumed, not having seen them leave. Oo-lors suggested a drink that she found much too sweet and heady, the music dinned, and the dance floor was too slick. They left before the first show.

"I am sorry you feel unwell," Oo-lors said in the underground car. His fingers massaged the back of her neck, and her headache began to recede. She would have liked to return the pressure of his other hand on hers, but the image of Elli was too vividly with her.

Morgan refused Oo-lors's offer to spend the night. She was not surprised at his move—she had been expecting it since they left the club—but she *was* surprised at the regret she felt. He bent his head to brush her lips with an intimation of a kiss, and she leaned toward him for a fraction of a second before she backed away.

Oo-lors did not press. Morgan agreed to more sightseeing the next day, but only if she could also visit a school

The children sat in orderly rows facing the machines, an electrode fastened to a metal band encircling each head. "Direct pleasure-pain stimulus," the teacher said. "Ninety-five percent retention after only one session."

"May I look closer?" Morgan indicated the small figure hunched over the console nearest her.

The child was insensible to her approach, but the teacher nodded.

The lesson on the screen was in Midian symbols, meaningless to Morgan. The technique, however, was familiar—negative reinforcement by electric shock, which had been barred on Terra for a decade before she had left. The child muttered softly to himself as he pressed keys in response to test questions, wincing with each error. He made few.

When he had completed the lesson successfully a light flashed on his screen and the teacher smilingly presented him with colored fruitbeads. "That will be your function," the Midian woman said to Morgan. "The children will always associate Terrans with pleasant rewards. A necessary response for a citizen of a tourist city."

Morgan knew better than to voice any disapproval. The technique, she understood, had worked well enough for rote learning, but had fallen into disrepute when challenged by humanitarians. A worse danger, though, had been the possibility of conditioning—which the Midians seemed to accept as a matter of course. She began to see them in a new light.

"What about the younger children—the non-readers?" she asked.

"Ah! The success rate with them is ninety-nine percent. This way, please." The silver-haired woman beamed.

Damn those smiles, Morgan thought, suddenly sick of the ubiquitous pleasantness. She followed the teacher into a soft-floored room where tiny sprites lolled and played quietly and slept, all wearing metal headbands and black-and-silver cylinders in their ears.

"Continuous exposure. These four-to-six-year-olds are the most impressionable of our students, and it is a joy to see them respond."

Morgan saw little response in the roomful of apathetic youngsters, but again she held her peace. The woman removed the cylinder from a doll-like figure little more than a baby and began to question her in Midian. The responses issued in fluted tones like a perfect recording.

"Our civil code," the woman said proudly. "You can be sure she will never act against it."

"Did you attend a school like that?" Morgan asked Oo-lors. They had rented a flitter to visit the offshore islands.

"Very similar. Mine was in the Oskerry tower, and we had a splendid view of the spaceport." He chuckled. "Half of us wanted to be pilots."

She watched as he handled the flitter with

more than common skill. "What happened? How did you get sidetracked?"

"Nothing happened. I showed an aptitude for languages, and my profile pointed me to a people-oriented profession."

"And you've been happy?"

"Never more than now." She saw herself reflected in his Midian eyes, and she could swear that he spoke without guile.

They landed and spent the day sailing. Oolors handled the boat, too, with more than common skill, and she gave up feeling sorry for him.

The day of sightseeing stretched into a week, then another. Morgan saw Elli only once, briefly, at a newcomers' luncheon on top of the Sirrikit tower. At first she did a double take. Elli was so expertly made up that even her freckles were hidden, and her tamed hair hung smoothly in silver loops.

Still, she did not look well. It was hard to tell in her Midian daydress if she had actually lost weight, but the haggard angles of her face suggested that she had been dieting strenuously. Morgan suspected that the layer of cosmetics hid dark circles beneath her eyes.

Elli was too edgy to sit with Morgan, even for a minute. "I'm looking for an apartment." she said, "and I wondered if you knew of anything in the Amasit. My tower seems to be all full." She searched the restaurant with quick nervous glances. "I can't talk to you now. Ai-won's getting a table, and I don't want to keep him waiting."

Morgan detained her with a hand on her arm. "Of course I'll find out," she said. "But tell me, how have you been? You're thinner, aren't you? Is it because of Ai-won?"

Satisfied that no one was looking for her, Elli perched on the edge of a chair. "No, he likes me

the way I am. It's just that . . . I feel like such a
lump beside him.''

Elli's feverish eyes and the imagined shadow
beneath her makeup still bothered Morgan. "How
is your money holding out?"

"I'm . . . all right." Her hesitation gave the lie
to her words.

"You know to call me if you ever need help."

Elli threw up her head.

"Or just to visit." God, she was touchy.

Ai-won beckoned and Elli ran, their matching
emerald pendants gleaming in the sun.

Morgan remained at her solitary table. She
had been seeing less of Oo-lors, by her design.
He hadn't earned much in commissions from
her, and though he professed not to mind she
knew that he had to make a living.

Perhaps he already had another client. She
felt a twinge of jealousy, though they had not
become lovers.

Almost every other newcomer was with an
aliti. Morgan knew that she should be spending
the week in bed with Oo-lors if she were to
follow custom. The self-satisfied smirks on the
faces of every returned visitor she had ever seen
had left no doubt as to what they considered the
chief charm of Midia.

Her Corps director on Cygni had been no ex-
ception. No wonder, Morgan thought, he had
failed to mention the nature of the schools.

It would be a long year without some form of
morphia, she knew. She toyed with her food,
thinking of Oo-lors. Perhaps she should call him.
After all, when in Rome . . .

What difference should it make that it was his
job? He was conditioned to love her. And as for
her, it wouldn't be hard to lose herself in those
eyes.

It didn't matter to Elli that Ai-won was an
aliti, Morgan thought. Maybe she was getting

her money's worth and Morgan was being the fool.

"It is un—uh—unusual to see offworld person alone."

The waiter's awkward Terran caused Morgan a start of surprise; most Midians were so fluent.

She recollected herself. "I don't mind being an oddball. Though you should have seen the consternation when I asked for a table for one."

He grinned. His forehead was tattooed with a round black spot, but there was also something more subtly different about him.

Another waiter came hurrying over. "Is everything all right, madam?" He spoke in rapid Midian to the black-spotted one, who withdrew. "It is unfortunate," he said to Morgan. "Two of our regular men were sick today, and the bureau sent that one. Has he been annoying you?"

"Not at all," she assured him. "The service has been excellent."

She didn't see the first waiter again until just before she left. As he came to clear her table he slipped a note beneath her folded scarf.

She read it in the elevator: "Help Midia," and a number to call.

She crumpled the note. No one was watching her, but she felt conspicuously branded herself. All she needed was to become involved in a conspiracy! The Corps rules against political involvement allowed no leeway, and Morgan hadn't worked her way up to seniority to be booted out for someone else's cause.

Still she kept the note in her fist, and when she was safely in her apartment she secreted it in an antique book.

She began to look more closely at the Midians on the public transports and in the less expensive stores. Very occasionally she saw others marked with the black circle.

She asked the vocom. "*Sorgots*," it replied. "The uneducated."

She keyed for further information and got the entire education code. Only one passage applied: "Those who for any reason fail to matriculate shall be visibly identified."

She asked Oo-lors, invited to dinner at her apartment. "We try to have nothing to do with them," he said. An expression of distaste crossed his face. "They have not been properly schooled."

"I don't understand. You mean they failed to graduate? I thought the machines could teach anyone."

"Anyone who gives them the opportunity. The *sorgots* have not enrolled, or have withdrawn early. Who knows why? Misguided parents, *sorgots* themselves, condemning their children to be outcasts." He shivered. "You must avoid them; they are unsafe."

"You mean dangerous? But they seem to move freely, everywhere."

"Unfortunately, yes. Unless they have actually committed a crime they cannot be restricted or reconditioned, but they always have the potential for antisocial behavior. And because it is difficult for them to find employment the risk from them is even greater."

"How do they live, then? I saw one working as a waiter."

"That was unusual. Most of them work at the tank farms or in the diamond mines. A good thing—it keeps them away from Trianka."

Oo-lors traced designs with his finger on the tablecloth. He seemed so uneasy with the topic that Morgan abandoned it. "Perhaps you can help me with something else," she said.

"Of course. Anything."

"I've been trying to locate an inexpensive apartment for Elli Trask; the one she's in costs a mint. I know there must be some here, but I can't get any information from the rental office because I'm an offworlder. They say I have to go through an *aliti*."

"Yes, it is the way things are done here. But Ai-won Mellinor is your friend's *aliti*, and he will take care of it for her. It would be most improper for me to interfere."

Oo-lors assumed the blandly innocent expression she had met with in the rental office. Morgan swore under her breath. One thing for sure, she was glad *she* wasn't at their mercy.

She brought in coffee, still in an ill humor. Oo-lors produced two fosstubes.

She relaxed in the sweet mist. He couldn't help it, she told herself. "I'm surprised you were free tonight," she said. "No new client yet?"

He affected shock. "How can you suggest such a thing?" He stroked her arm lightly, his face intent and somewhat sad. "It will take me longer than a few weeks to get over you."

Perhaps it was wishful thinking, but again she was almost positive that he spoke the truth.

Morgan reported, finally, to her school. She hated it as much as she had thought she would, but the hours were short and the pleasures of Trianka waited just outside the tower. She had always loved sea sports, and she also quickly became adept at airsailing. Oo-lors continued to accompany her, unremunerated, and she began to think that she had misjudged him.

Elli, however, did not get on as well. She visited Morgan, still expensively dressed and holding stiffly to her pride, but she sipped coffee from a cup that shook.

"I don't know why I'm so nervous." Her laugh was brittle. "Too many hi-flyers, I guess, and not enough sleep."

Elli was now noticeably thinner. Something in her eyes, however, hinted of a deeper anxiety

than could be caused by diet pills or dissipa-
tion. Morgan prodded her gently. "It's more than
that. You're in trouble, Elli. Tell me."

Elli put down the cup and clasped her hands.
Her armor began to crack. "Oh, it's nothing
very bad. Only—I haven't been able to find a
cheaper apartment."

"If that's all—you can move in with me. At
least for a while."

"No, I couldn't do that. You see, Ai-won is
living with me now." Still, she looked around
Morgan's four rooms longingly, as if she could
somehow make another bedroom appear.

"No, in that case it wouldn't work," Morgan
agreed. "But are you sure you can't find anything? Surely Ai-won . . .'"

"He's checked all the lower floors of the towers, and even out of town, and he says there's
nothing available." She slumped into the couch
pillows, no longer bothering to hide her desperation. "I can't even pay next month's rent!"

"I can give you a loan."

"Thanks, but that wouldn't really help. I've
got to find work. I've looked everywhere, and
they only want to hire Midians.

"Morgan, do you think you could get me on at
your school?" She sat up, pleading. "Don't they
use teachers' aides or anything like that? Or I
could help coach the kids in Terran."

Morgan couldn't bear to tell her that she was
little more than an aide herself and that the
languages were all sleeptaught. She promised
Elli to see what she could do.

Of course she had no success. "Your friend
can always ship out to one of the colonies,"
Morgan's head teacher said. "Recruiters come
through here often. It's either that, or go to the
diamond mines."

Elli chose the mines. She came to store some
things at Morgan's apartment the night before

she was to leave. She was pale and more tightly wound than ever, but determined.

Morgan tried to dissuade her. "You're going in blind," she said. "You don't know anything about diamond mining."

"So what! It doesn't seem to bother anyone except you. They'll show me how to set charges. It's what I'll be doing, and they tell me it's easy to learn."

"It also sounds dangerous. You could be hurt, or killed."

Elli squared her jaw. "You can't talk me out of it, Morgan. I've signed a contract."

Morgan cast about in desperation. "But what does Ai-won say?"

"He wants me to stay on Midia, and it's the only way."

Elli did not return after a month for her scheduled leave. Morgan checked with the vocom and was given a number at the mines. The office there reported her still in the field, and Morgan left a message.

She called every day for a week, until finally the vocom stated that Elli Trask was no longer listed.

The computer resisted all her efforts to elicit further information. Finally Oo-lors, under pressure, pulled some strings and got her connected to a manager at the mines.

"An unfortunate accident," he said coldly. "But Trask was informed of the risks. We have her waiver."

"Why wasn't I told? Surely someone found my messages?"

"The only person we had on record to notify was Ai-won Mellinor."

She felt the beginnings of a burning anger. "I suppose he collected any death benefits?"

"That is privileged information."

He cut her off and she stared at the blank visiplate. For confirmation of her suspicions she grilled the vocom until it divulged what she sought—the finder's fee for recruiting a new mine worker. It was a sizable amount.

She set up an appointment with Ai-won through his service, pretending to be a newly arrived tourist. She chose the most public spot in Trianka—the harbor restaurant at midday.

She waited at the bar until Ai-won walked in, beautiful as an angel with his floating silver hair and his glowing eyes. He wore Elli's diamonds in his ears.

He looked around expectantly, saw her, and started.

She had planned to play him slowly and make him squirm, but hate exploded in her. She threw her drink in his face and rushed out.

That evening she called the number on the note.

2

The meeting was in a subbasement of the Sirrikit. "You are quite sure no one saw you come here?" A gray-haired Terran woman in a work coverall drew Morgan quickly inside.

"No, I was careful." Morgan blinked to accommodate her vision to the dim light of the cavelike room. Six men and three women sat around a rough trestle table. All but one—the Terran—bore the tattoed mark of the *sorgots*.

"Good. If you are suspected you will lose all usefulness to us. It's fortunate that your little 'incident' with the *aliti* Mellinor was no more than that—something that could be passed off as a lovers' spat."

"I wanted to claw his eyes out."

"You'll get your chance for a more constructive revenge."

Introductions were made. The Terran woman, Alison Pease, was the tenant of the basement room. She had been like Morgan a disenchanted visitor. She had stayed to help the *sorgot* cause, had married one and seen him lost to the mines. I-lit Saarin, the waiter, was with his wife and his two brothers. They made Morgan welcome in broken Terran. A man with one arm was a disabled miner, and the other three, Midians so old and desiccated that their parchmentlike skin seemed stretched over nothing but bone, were introduced with respect as elders. The old ones glowered at Morgan and mumbled something in their own language.

"They don't trust you," Alison said. "If you betray us, it'll be on my head. Mine and I-lit's."

"I not worry," I-lit said. "I know at once she is—how you say—'prospect,' she with no *aliti*."

"I certainly won't betray you," Morgan said. "But I'd like to know just what I'm getting into. Are you revolutionaries? How many *sorgots* are there, and what kind of a chance do you have against millions of conditioned-to-the-teeth Midians?"

"None at all, at the moment," Alison admitted. "And there aren't enough of us for any kind of an open revolt. All we want to do now is start to break down that conditioning so that maybe in ten or twenty years there *will* be enough doubters to do something. Your friend Elli Trask was one unfortunate in an all-too-long line, but an even greater tragedy is the fact that Ai-won Mellinor was deliberately programmed to be what he is.

"And that's where you can help us."

"Yes, I'd like to. But it can't be anything overt. I'd lose my job."

"Don't worry; it *has* to be secret."

"What is it that I'd be doing?"

Alison looked around the group and spoke rapidly in Midian. The four Saarins and the miner nodded, and so, after a moment, did the elders.

"We need access to the teaching disks. If we can modify enough of them—perhaps even have you slip in a couple of our own to the younger kids—it's bound to put a bug in that conditioning. Don't worry—it can't be anything too radical, because the minute it's detected we're through. But I understand the teachers don't review the material or even pay much attention to it. Isn't that right?"

Morgan nodded. "We're nothing but a bunch of button-pushers. We set up the kids at the machines, and that's the extent of our 'teaching.'" The more she thought about the proposal, which at first had seemed harebrained, the more feasible it appeared. She felt a rising excitement. "It just might work. The kids are so used to accepting unquestioningly whatever comes out of the machines that I don't think they'd betray any surprise if you threw in the whole Free Worlds Charter. It ought to start them thinking later on, when the pressure of all the memorizing they have to do is off."

I-lit grinned. "I tell you, she the one."

"I-lit's father went to a government school for eight years," Alison said. "It was a teacher from Esperanza who opened his eyes and saved him and his family from the assembly-line brainwash."

"A government school?" Morgan wondered at the term. "You mean there's any other kind?"

"How do you think these four managed to get themselves educated?" Alison indicated the young Saarins. "All *sorgots* aren't the illiterate clods your Midian friends would have you believe. I-lit and his brothers are computechs—a family trade, not that they're allowed to practice it—

and Kalen's a poet who works in a laundry. We have our own underground schools. Not much hardware, of course, but at least we don't produce robots."

Morgan turned to I-lit. "So you learned Terran without sleeptapes?"

"Not so good, eh? But you bring lesson disks and I fix up nobody tell. Sure, lotsa ways get into school circuits. Lotsa us people got ideas mess up programs good."

"Too many ideas," Alison said with a grimace. "Don't worry though, Morgan; I'll see that it's not too fiery and that it fits in smoothly."

"I wasn't worried," Morgan said. It wasn't wholly true. She felt easier than she had since Elli's death, but all the same, she didn't want to become a martyr. "Just out of curiosity, what happened to that teacher from Esperanza?"

They all laughed.

Morgan, however, wanted an answer. "Seriously."

Alison shrugged. "As far as we know, she went back to her homeworld with some odd memories."

One of the older men spoke sharply to Alison in Midian, and from then on the meeting proceeded in that language. Morgan sat uncomprehending, cursing the Corps director who had assured her that all Midians spoke fluent Terran and that there was no need to learn the native tongue.

Alison threw her an occasional quick explanation. They were discussing the infants' school, housing needs for a new *sorgot* couple, conditions at the mines, and the latest death statistics. Frequent arguments punctuated the talk, O-lit and I-lit Saarin at one point shouting and almost coming to blows.

Alison calmed them. "It's the frustration," she said to Morgan. "So little we can do."

"I like to hear it," Morgan said. She couldn't imagine Oo-lors ever shouting in anger.

The brothers eventually appeared to reach an accord. The meeting broke up around midnight, the participants leaving singly and in twos. Morgan received a warm handclasp from each one.

Alison detained her. "It would be better for you to wait a half hour or so."

"Good. I'd like a chance to talk."

Alison made a gesture of apology. "I'd offer you something to eat, but my cooking facilities are limited." She pointed to a portable heat ring. "Maybe a cup of tea?"

"No thanks." Morgan looked around the sparsely furnished studio. "Do you really live here?"

"Some of the time. I move around a lot, organizing our people. I'm afraid I'm what we Terrans used to call a rabble-rouser." Alison moved the lamps to one end of the table and pulled out a more comfortable chair from a corner. When Morgan declined it she sank into it herself.

In the brighter light Morgan saw a small, wiry woman who had the appearance of one aged more by a harsh life than by years. Her skin was etched with fine wrinkles, and her hair, gray around her face but dark in the back, was thick and abundant. Her eyes were small and blue and piercing.

She smiled at Morgan, a myriad of tiny lines fanning her cheeks. "I know you must be curious about me, so I'll save you the embarrassment of asking. I came here thirty years ago, when I was a head-in-the-clouds kid just out of college. A vacation, paid for by my father—yes, he could well afford it—to lure me away from what he considered an unsuitable match with a barefoot truthseeker.

"Daddy had been here himself, and knew what sort of distractions I'd find." She made a wry

SEVEN WORLDS

face. "Poor man, he should have left well enough alone. I didn't fall in love with my *aliti*; I fell in love with my houseboy."

"So you stayed. The money from home kept coming?"

"For a while, until he found out and cut it off. Then we had to scramble for a living, like all the other *sorgots*. Ro-han lost his houseboy job, of course, and we panned the riverbeds for a number of years. But then the mining guilds got tough with us free prospectors—not that they ever paid us fairly for the few chips we brought in—and closed the market to us. Ro-han had to go to work in the mines."

Morgan sat up straight. "Tell me about them. How he died, and how Elli died."

Alison half-closed her eyes and seemed to shrink into her chair. Her voice, when she started to speak, was edged with bitterness. "It's Midia's well-kept secret—the cost of those diamonds. Tourists don't visit the mines. Or most Midians, either. It's one place *sorgots* can always find work. The guilds have to hire them and ignorant offworlders like your friend to undertake the more dangerous tasks. Blasting new shafts, in particular. Luring them with generous bonuses they seldom live to collect." Her hands gripped the arms of her chair as she controlled herself with an obvious effort.

Morgan waited. "What is it that causes the danger? I mean, more than in other mining situations?"

"It's the rock. *Ferklith*, we call it. Fire-rock. It's comparable to kimberlite, on Earth, only denser. The *ferklith* is under such stress that it's hard to control the explosions. Sometimes it starts a chain reaction that closes entire tunnels.

"Our ancient volcanoes were caldrons of pressure, and our pipes are richer in diamonds than even the Big Mouth on Vulcan. Midian Mining

controls the output to maintain prices and demand, and fortunately for us"—her mouth twisted—"we always have enough desperate people
to go into those pipes."

Alison stared bleakly at Morgan, her eyes hard
diamonds themselves. "There was nothing left
of Ro-han to bury after the explosion. Let's hope
your friend Elli died as quickly. Sometimes they
don't."

The two women sat in silence for a long moment. Morgan finally spoke. "Aren't there ...
safety measures that can be used? How about
waldos?"

"What, all that expense when we have too
many *sorgots* anyway? Besides, the mine workers have signed waivers. Who cares about them?"
Alison pulled herself out of her chair and angrily turned off the lamps, all but one. "No, we
can't hope for anything without reeducation, and
that's why you're so valuable to us. Too valuable to risk discovery. You'd better go now, and
for God's sake don't attract any attention."

Morgan slipped out of the Sirrikit through a
service entrance and joined the evening stroll-
ers. She took a flitter to the harbor for a cover-
up drink and pretended to be slightly tipsy when
she returned to the Amasit.

The green light flashed on Ilia Lammi's monitor. Morgan composed her face into the expected
smile and reached for the jar of fruitbeads.

Ilia's eyes glistened with an added luster.
Greed, perhaps, or triumph—she had been struggling with the lesson for two hours. She chose a
purple *kivit* and basked in the approval of Morgan and headmistress Firkin.

Ilia looked to be about ten years old, but Morgan knew that she might well be in her teens;
the Midian children were so small that she com-
monly misjudged their ages. Ilia's complexion

was translucent porcelain and her delicate bones suggested the fragility of a Dresden figurine. The young girl looked forward to being an *aliti*, she had once told Morgan in her computer-perfect sleeptaught Terran.

Ilia had completed an entire program, and the headmistress removed her headband and sent her to play while she selected a new disk for the machine. Morgan noted the number of the completed one, and unobstrusively checked the programs of the other students in the room. None of them would be using that particular disk for several weeks.

She had no idea what lesson Ilia had just had impressed upon her. Neither, apparently, did Firkin, who followed a numbered chart and seldom looked at the screens. Morgan wondered, as she always did, just what it was she had rewarded. It would be something quite different, she knew, the next time the disk was used.

Morgan removed three teaching disks and a half-dozen sleeptapes that day. "They won't be missed for at least a week," she whispered to Kalen Saarin, handing over the software in a bundle of dirty laundry.

"Yes. I get to you . . . three days." Kalen disappeared into a steamy back room with the bundle, and another laundress, a non-*sorgot*, appeared to punch in Morgan's billing.

Morgan delivered more on successive days, replacing the altered ones when her laundry came back. The exchange was suspended for a week when Kalen was transferred to the Maiku tower, and resumed when O-lit began to scrub floors at the Amasit. Alison and Morgan passed one another each day at a prearranged time on the pedway and exchanged signals that all was well.

Morgan was on tenterhooks the day the first modified disk was used. She was fortunately the only teacher in the classroom—Firkin would surely have noticed how frequently the Terran glanced at one particular screen even though the Midian symbols were meaningless to her.

Morgan expected a gasp or a shout at any moment. She projected the visit from the angry parents, the disclosure, the denunciation. She saw herself expelled from Midia and washed out of the Corps. She wondered what in all of space she could have been thinking of.

The first hour went by, however, and nothing happened. The student revealed no surprise at the content of his lesson, nor did he seem to experience any unusual difficulty with it. He winced a few times during the testing, restudied, and achieved success on his second try.

This time Morgan's smile was genuine, and she even allotted an extra bead.

"You seem in unusually good spirits this evening." Oo-lors twirled Morgan around on the dance floor of the Crystal Cave. He moved with a light sureness that set her own feet to skimming. She had never felt so graceful.

"It's the school. I must be getting used to it. At least, I had a good day today."

"I am glad." The music changed its beat, and he pulled her into the circle of his arms. "I know you have not been satisfied with it up to now. It has distressed me."

She looked up at him in surprise. "I didn't know you realized how I felt. But of course— you're sensitive to auras."

"You remembered! Perhaps there is hope for me yet." They swayed with the music, the lengths of their bodies touching. "I am happy, too, being with you again. It has been much too long."

Alison had cautioned Morgan to keep up normal appearances, so she had finally returned Oo-lors's calls. The *aliti* seemed to be unchanged in his affections, though he had begun to take on new clients. His present ones were an elderly Elyrian couple, he said, who didn't care for night life. "A few balloon rides, a lot of shopping. Easy to satisfy, and I still have my evenings free."

They joined a table of Oo-lor's friends: Jallis, who cut diamonds, and Ariane and Ah-nor, who did nothing at all with dedicated fervor. Ah-nor, who had been speaking, switched easily from Midian to Terran when Morgan sat down. "The thermals will be early this season. Ariane and I are planning a month of gliding. Can you all join us?"

Jallis squealed and clapped her hands. "I have not been for a . . . for an . . . age." She dimpled and grinned at Morgan. "Is that the correct word for a very long time?"

Morgan assured her that it was. Ah-nor fingered a faint scar above his right ear. "You should get an implant, Jallis. It's marvelous—you never have to fumble for a word."

Jallis made a face. "Ten thousand credits?"

"You will excuse me, please," she said to Morgan, then let loose a stream of what sounded like affectionate teasing, in Midian, at Ah-nor.

"A biochip?" Morgan asked Oo-lors. She had never heard of one for such casual use.

"There is nothing Ah-nor does not have," Oo-lors said.

Morgan could believe it. The crystal sheets on the cave walls drew fire from the diamonds that glittered on the wealthy Midian's neck and arms. They were sitting at the same booth where Elli had once sought reckless pleasure. It was an unfortunate coincidence.

"Can you take a week off to go gliding?" Oo-lors pressed her hand; the others were absorbed in their own conversation. "You could see the south coast, and with Ah-nor we would sleep every night in a silk tent. There would be no hardships."

"Oh, I could get the time, all right," Morgan said. "I haven't even begun to use my vacation allowance. But what I'd rather do is ... visit the diamond mines. Do you think that could be arranged?"

Oo-lors started. "I had hoped you had forgotten that distressing business about your friend." A wary look appeared in his eyes.

Morgan caught herself. "No, it has nothing to do with Elli," she assured him. "I'm interested, is all. And I'd like to get some holos so I can bore my students someday on another planet."

"You can buy excellent holos."

"I know, but it's not the same. What's the problem? If it's too difficult ..."

Oo-lor's face revealed the conflict between his own inclinations and his training as an *aliti*. The training won. "I will see what I can do," he said.

He could not oblige her, however. "Midian Mining will allow no visitors at this time," he reported to Morgan the next day. "They are blasting, and the area is closed.

"You would not have liked it anyway," he said in a placating tone. "No one goes there. The mountains are hot and unpleasant, and there are no guest facilities. It would have been a tiresome trip. You will enjoy the gliding much more. Shall I tell Ah-nor that we will join him?"

Why not? she thought. She had to pretend to be a proper pleasure-loving Midian. And as she had said, she was due for a leave.

The wind seemed to enter Morgan through her pores and fill her until she had no weight. She rode the steady current with outspread arms that were one with the wings of her glider, dipping and soaring in an ecstasy of freedom.

Below her, green fields unrolled from small wooded hills, with here and there dots of cattle. She caught a downdraft and swooped low to startle a band of woolly *kaffirs*. A manor house appeared, a rambling stone pile; figures waved from a sunroof.

Beyond a fringe of forest she glimpsed the ocean. Ahead of her Oo-lors signaled and made a turn.

The eddies over the water were strong and erratic. Morgan felt her way between them to a slow airstream where she could glide without being buffeted. She drifted over the line of beach until she spotted the bright tents of their camp.

Oo-lors was on the ground, and Jallis was making an awkward landing. Morgan circled at a safe distance while the Midian woman fought the crossdrafts. When it was her own turn she angled low below the turbulence and came in on a slant that skimmed the waves.

"A smooth landing!" Oo-lors ran up to help her unbuckle. "Those currents are tricky coming down, but in the morning we can launch from the bluff."

The tents were pitched on a sandy cove sheltered by a steep headland. They had been flying all day, and Ah-nor's servant had set up the camp. It consisted of one large tent and two smaller ones, with rugs spread between them.

Ah-nor came out of the big tent, carrying glasses filled with a green liquid. "We'll have dinner in an hour, in here. But first—to day one!"

"Fair currents and fairer partners," said Oo-lors, smiling at Morgan and holding up his glass.

"To flying. It was incredible!" Morgan clinked glasses and sipped. Her face burned where the goggles had not protected it and her upper arms were a dull ache, but she was still under the euphoric spell of the wind.

The tongue-numbing drink immediately eased the worst of her discomfort. "Pure magic," she declared, twisting her shoulders with no twinges.

"You'll feel even better after a warm bath," Ah-nor said. "It's waiting in your tent." He pointed to the rainbow-hued bubble that flew a Terran banner.

Oo-lors guided her, and she felt that she needed both of his arms around her to anchor her to the ground. Then, in the tent, she needed them for quite another reason. Alison and the *sorgots* were in another world, and in this one she knew only her awakened sensations and the beautiful man who wanted her as much as she did him.

The water in the hip bath grew cold while they gave mutual pleasure on the silk-covered mat. Morgan followed Oo-lor's lead deliriously as he utilized every possible contact of their bodies. She had never been a moaner or a shouter, but this time she cried out in her final throes, and his own gasped sounds joined hers in a wild sort of paean.

When the last throb had stilled to a velvety peace she lay snug in his arms and smiled.

"How do you feel?" His breath fluttered on her cheek.

She moved her head to allow his lips the hollow of her throat. "You know." A laugh bubbled out unbidden. *More magic*. Did she think it or say it? No matter, he would understand.

His arms tightened around her.

They missed dinner with Ah-nor and the others, but it was waiting in covered dishes when Oo-lors finally opened the doorflap of their tent. They remained secluded until morning, and Morgan learned the *aliti*'s body as she had never been able to fathom his mind. The sex was the best she had known. It was all true—all the extravagant claims—and she had the added satisfaction of knowing that she was no client.

In the morning, at breakfast with the group, there was no need for embarrassment; it was clear that Ah-nor had shared his tent with both Midian women. Ariane still lolled half dressed on the cushions of the bedmat, and the contents of Jallis's pack were scattered everywhere.

"I'm going for a swim," Ariane announced languidly. "Save me some rolls and *mistiril*." She walked naked out of the tent.

Ariane had the thin, hairless body of a child, but with tiny pink-tipped breasts. The effect was a sensuality as strong as it was subtle.

"Would you like to go too?" Oo-lors asked.

Morgan shook her head. Not and face a comparison.

He squeezed her hand and pressed it against his chest. She could feel his heart, and was reassured. For whatever the reason, she knew she had no cause for unease or jealousy as far as he was concerned.

They left the disordered camp for the unseen servants to pack up and move. "Only a four-hour flight, this time," Ah-nor said. "Our muscles will get toned just enough, and we'll have the afternoon to relax at a lagoon and a hot spring."

Morgan flew at Oo-lors's side, unwilling to be separated by more than the margin of safety. When the wind filled her she thought only of him: the chiseled perfection of his features, the quirk of his mouth, the slender lines of his body, his hands. All of his physical being was so etched on her consciousness that as she gave herself to the currents it seemed that she must be strung as finely as the flax of a piper reed, her nerves as exquisitely honed.

When they landed they repaired to their tent again immediately, and only when their passion was sated did they relax in the steamy water of the mineral spring.

The five naked figures floated idly, buoyed by the heavy water. Jallis and Ariane chattered in a mixture of Terran and Midian: the air currents and what they wanted for dinner and gossip about people Morgan didn't know. Ah-nor pulled himself out of the spring and paraded its circumference before he left for a dip in the lagoon. He was well endowed, Morgan saw, but no more so than Oo-lors.

Morgan had been conscious of their host's eyes on her all the time she bathed. When he returned he paddled next to Oo-lors for a whispered conference, still looking her way.

Oo-lors shook his head with vehemence and Ah-nor kicked himself away. He floated past Morgan with a regretful smile.

"Of course he wanted you," Oo-lors said later, when they were alone. "And of course I said no."

"Why didn't he speak to me himself?" Morgan asked. Then: "Oh, never mind, I know the answer. You're the friend, and you'll be here long after I'm gone."

"Partly," he agreed. "But also he did not want to offend you if you were not inclined toward him. Was I wrong in turning him down for you?"

She demonstrated her answer without the need for words, to the satisfaction of them both.

When Oo-lors was asleep she thought of Alison, who had also loved a Midian. How much had glands to do with her politics? Then she dismissed the thought as unworthy. She had better watch herself, she cautioned, and keep her pleasures apart from the rational part of her brain. Otherwise she could become someone whom the old Morgan would not recognize.

It was easy not to think at all for the remainder of the week. They rode the winds every day, following the coast, and their luxurious camp was waiting for them each night. The Midians, at least to Morgan, spoke only of trivial matters. She was determined to learn the language, and Oo-lors, with more enthusiasm than method, threw himself into teaching her. The lessons invariably led to mispronounced endearments and laughter, then to a language that needed no translation.

For their last night they eschewed the tent to sleep under the stars in a moss-floored glade. The soft voices of Ah-nor and his partners drifted from another clearing, and from the trees something nocturnal hummed a refrain that was almost a song.

Morgan could scarcely breathe for the tight pain in her chest. It was an interlude, she knew; not the stuff of reality. Still, her eyes filled at the thought of tomorrow.

"When we go back, this does not have to end," Oo-lors whispered.

Morgan did not answer. She knew that with her underground activities the liaison would be difficult to maintain. She knew it was crazy to make herself vulnerable at this time. She knew what Alison would say, but she couldn't give Oo-lors up. Somehow, she had to compartmentalize her life.

Ah-nor's man returned Morgan and Oo-lors to Trianka by flitter; the others were to continue their gliding for two more weeks. Ah-nor thanked Morgan as if her company were a rare gift, and Jallis and Ariane kissed her and called her "sister."

Back in Trianka, at the school, the mannerly children welcomed her with flowers. Firkin, too, appeared to have missed her. Morgan could perceive none of them as victims, and it wasn't until she visited the infants' room that she felt any resurgence of her crusading zeal.

In her own classroom, she tested her new language skills by attempting to read some of the lessons on the screens. The simpler ones—the only ones she could decipher at all—were rife with large-lettered slogans. She recognized repeatedly the symbols for Midian Mining. "Midian Mining Protects" headed each page of what appeared to be an elementary history lesson.

Her perspective shifted back to the time before her vacation. She went to the files, to see if there were any disks that could be removed. Firkin came into the room and Morgan returned to her desk. Apparently no one suspected her, but she would have to maintain her guard.

She contacted Alison, who arranged for a meeting.

They picked over the fruit at a crowded market in the Amasit center while they worked out a new plan for the disk exchanges. Alison looked drawn. A tic, which Morgan had not noticed before, twitched in the hollow of one cheek. "I suppose *that one* will be hanging around you all the time now," she said, frowning.

"No," Morgan said. "He wanted to move in, but I persuaded him against it."

The answer failed to clear Allison's brow. The women moved off in opposite directions and met again at the displays of offworld products. Morgan sniffed at an orange. "I can't afford these, but I can't resist them, either."

"Our *muscales* are just as good," Alison said.

Morgan dropped the orange into the delivery slot and punched her code. "We all need some indulgences." She met Alison's gaze. "I can control mine."

Alison sighed. The tic twitched again. "Come to my place tonight," she whispered before she moved into the carryout line.

*   *   *

Alison's room was hot and airless. Morgan had spent an hour covering her tracks in the summer crowds, and she arrived sweating.

It was not another policy meeting. Except for a figure reclining on a corner cot, Alison was alone.

Morgan pulled the fabric of her tunic away from her skin. She hoped Alison's business was important. "So what is this about? I thought it was too risky for me to come here."

Alison handed her a glass of lukewarm tea. "I wanted you to meet Hafla, who's staying with me." She motioned to the *sorgot* woman on the cot, who rose and came hesitantly into the light. "She had to leave her job at the veg tanks in Evor Valley."

Morgan could not suppress a gasp. Huge flaky puckerings scored the skin of Hafla's face, and her hands resembled the withered claws of a bird. Alison pulled off the woman's scarf to reveal a scalp similarly afflicted, with only patches of hair remaining.

Morgan's own skin turned clammy. She stuttered a Midian greeting, then turned to Alison. "What happened to her?"

Alison smiled grimly. "The latest wonder product of Evor's labs. It's a new chemical that's added to the sludge in the tanks. Really zips up the growth."

"It did *that* to her? But then . . . what are we eating?"

Alison snorted. "Don't worry, the food's perfectly safe. The only danger is to the workers who do the fertilizing. And of course, they're all *sorgots*."

Alison paced the length of the room, her voice rising. "I wanted you to see this, to realize what it is we're fighting. Your playmate Oo-lors, he's as dangerous as any of them. *We can't afford to make mistakes now!"* She clenched her fist and pounded the table until it threatened to collapse.

Hafla edged back to her corner, her eyes wide with alarm. Morgan was shaken, too, but not in the way Alison had intended. She was disturbed by an Alison she hadn't seen before, a zealot whose fiery anger was directed at her.

Unjustly. "I don't understand why you're so upset," Morgan said. "Oo-lors is a perfect cover. And you're the one who told me to act like any other offworlder. It would have been suspicious for me to keep turning him down."

"You could have ... you didn't have to ... oh, don't you see, it's too risky. This is no game we're playing. I don't know what Oo-lors means to you, but he can't be as important as the future of Midia. If you were really with us, you'd sacrifice your bed romps."

Morgan could feel the heat of anger in her own face, but she held herself stiffly in check. "I don't see how my private life has anything to do with helping the *sorgots*. It's something completely separate."

"You may think so, but the truth is that you aren't in control any longer. You're lost, *lost!*" Alison continued to pace, furiously, and to glare at Morgan.

You're the one who's lost, Morgan thought. She wondered for the first time what it was she had gotten herself into. She couldn't pull out now—wouldn't want to—but her confidence in Alison's leadership was being sorely tried.

Something in Morgan's expression drew Alison up short. She stopped her pacing, sat down with careful movements, and rested her arms on the table. She studied Morgan over the tips of steepled fingers. "Perhaps I misjudged you."

It was enough of an apology for Morgan. "I haven't changed," she assured Alison. "I'm still with you." She looked toward Hafla on the bed. "I didn't need to be primed with more horrors."

"Maybe not, but you ought to know everything. Hafla is a relative of the Saarins. The brothers won't be held back any longer, they're going to destroy that lab."

"Good. Though I don't suppose it'll really stop anything. There are other labs, aren't there?"

"Yes, and other tank farms. The *sorgots* will only be subjected to worse treatment." The tic in Alison's cheek began to jump. "On top of that, I find out that you've spent a week with some of the most seductive Midians in Trianka." She managed a tight smile. "Can you blame me for worrying?"

"Don't. I told you, I can't afford to get into any trouble. I'll be careful. You should have seen the circuitous route I took getting here. As for Oo-lors, I'll say it again: he's another part of my life entirely."

"Let's hope it stays that way."

Morgan was determined that it would. She encouraged Oo-lors to return to his Elyrian couple, while she continued smuggling disks and tapes and even bookspools to the *sorgots*. The doctored ones were all in use, and so far had created no ripple on the smooth-surfaced efficiency of the school.

She was transferred to another school, to allow more children the benefit of her smiles and rewards. When the Evor lab was sabotaged and I-lit captured and sent to a reconditioning center, Alison only stepped up their activities.

Morgan led a fractured life: theater parties and sumptuous dinners with Oo-lors and his friends, and hurried meetings with *sorgots* who lived on the edge of hunger. She attended fashion shows with Ariane while haunted by visions of Hafla's ruined face.

Oo-lors sensed her tension, but she persuaded

him that it was her work, that she had to adjust to the new school. He was so perceptive to her moods that she knew with a part of her mind that Alison was right.

However, she could no longer do without him. She tried to rationalize. Why shouldn't she enjoy Oo-lors's love? She wouldn't be any more useful to the *sorgots* by playing the martyr. Oo-lors was beautiful and passionate and sensitive; everything that was best about the Midians. If he represented the product of an abhorrent system, it was not his fault. His regard for her, though it may have been inspired by conditioning, was as real as anything he knew.

All this she told herself, but it didn't alter the truth that her will was no longer her own. When she most needed to be sharp and clear-headed, she had entered into the morass of an emotional entanglement. During the day she played her secret seditious game, and at night she slept in Oo-lors's arms; and sometimes when she awoke she couldn't remember who she was.

Not since she had been a teenager on Terra had she felt so torn. Then, it had been a contest between Davy Kingman, who had made her last year in the government dorm a miracle of awakening, and her determination to pass the Academy exams.

Ambition had won. It always had, up to now. Why, at this point in her life, had she succumbed to irrationality? She knew what the psychologists would say, about biological clocks and shaded zones, and she couldn't deny that she was beginning to count years. Not that she would have wanted a child by a Midian. The most she could produce with Oo-lors, and that only with laboratory help, would be a sterile offspring; but perhaps she needed to be reminded of her still viable femaleness.

Oo-lors reminded her of it constantly. His Elyrian couple left, but he seemed in no hurry to engage new clients. The more distracted Morgan appeared, the more he devoted himself to her, waiting for her each day after work and claiming every weekend. She no longer deluded herself that the affair was for her protection and that she could call it off whenever she wanted.

It was imperative, however, that she have more room. She tried to explain it to him without offense.

She failed. "Oh. I have been . . . pushing myself? You grow weary of me?" The hurt in his eyes wounded her.

She repeated. "No, I didn't mean that at all. It's just that . . . I'm something of a maverick. You know how I was when you first met me. I'm used to spending more time alone."

He still looked as though she had slapped him. "Forget it," she said. "I don't know what's wrong with me lately. Maybe I'm homesick. Too much of the good life here. Have you ever heard of anyone having a surfeit of Midia?"

His color returned, and his smile. "Yes, I believe it is possible. And the cure is simple—a drastic change. Do you still wish to visit the black mountains?"

"The mines? Of course I do! But I understood the area was closed."

"No, the operation is open again to visitors. I was notified some days ago, but I thought that perhaps you had given up the idea." He made a shamefaced moue of apology. "Hoped, actually. I admit I was not going to tell you. But now—I have changed my mind. I cannot believe you would enjoy it, but it would certainly be a novelty."

"You needn't come. I know how you feel about it."

"I would not think of letting you go alone. No, the expedition will be good for me, too. A different sort of experience."

3

Oo-lors booked passage on a transcontinental balloon that made a stop at the mining town of Ferrano. It was a leisurely six-hour trip, no power and drifting with the breeze. The passengers sipped drinks in the lounge and dined beside expansive windows while the countryside unfolded below.

It was flat country: rolling expanses of what looked like untouched fields and forests, broken only by an occasional manicured estate. They passed over a city of small towers that bordered a lake. Behind it stretched a complex of low, glass-roofed buildings that reminded Morgan of what had happened to Hafla and to I-lit.

"There's so much land," she said to Oo-lors. "Why do you need the veg tanks at all?"

Surprise froze his fork in mid air. "But farming is so ugly."

"I've never thought of it like that."

"Of course it is." He put down the fork and gestured with his hands. "Digging up grass, felling trees. All that damage to the land. Then the . . . the fertilizing and the cultivating and whatever it is they have to do, all of it out in the open. The smells. The machines. The *sorgots*." A grimace of distaste crossed his face. "Inefficient, too. It is so much better to keep it concentrated, as in those covered buildings down there, so the rest of Midia can remain a park. It is our responsibility to preserve the land in its beauty."

The land in its beauty. It was one of the slogans she had seen on the classroom monitors.
Oo-lors had learned well, Morgan thought. She
could not be angry with him, only impatient.
And when she considered the aesthetic depriva-
tion he was willing to undergo on this trip, she
overcame even that.

So far, though, there had been only luxury.
The meal was superb. In the sky, a flock of
puffbirds accompanied the balloon, flying in mea-
sured formation with the sun glinting through
their transparent wings.

Morgan refused a second dessert. "I thought
this was supposed to be a Spartan trip," she
said. "When do the hardships start?"

"Look over there."

She followed Oo-lors's gaze to the dark peaks
on the approaching horizon. The balloon caught
a fast current and the mountains rushed to meet
them, convoluted folds of black rock that had
risen from the earth, the steward explained, as
the spew from a primordial upheaval.

In a declivity between two barren ridges they
came to the mining area. They hung for a time
while the passengers exclaimed over the ugli-
ness: bare rocky earth scoured with gouges and
deep craters, heaps of refuse and abandoned,
falling-down buildings. Oo-lors pointed out a
gorge with a stream at its base. Newer structures, long and low, spread over a nearby plateau. "That must be the mine they are operating
now. The one we will visit."

The balloon began to move again, and the
steward announced their approach to Ferrano.
Morgan and Oo-lors collected their personal effects and joined the half-dozen others who were
to disembark.

They spent little time at Ferrano, a honky-
tonk city with a plethora of bars. Oo-lors en-

gaged a room at the hotel and rented a flitter to take them back to the mountains.

After a rough flight they landed on the plateau, at the headquarters site. A single unpaved street was lined with boxlike wooden buildings. The sun beat down fiercely, and there was no shade.

Oo-lors's face was tight as he helped her out. "I told you it would be unpleasant," he said.

Morgan agreed. She put on a sun visor, but there was no protection from the gritty dust that settled on her immediately. They headed for the nearest building.

It appeared to be a mess hall, unoccupied at the moment. Oo-lors found the kitchen, where a *sorgot* cook directed them to the mining office.

It was at the end of the street. "Someone should have been here to meet us," Oo-lors grumbled as they picked their way over the ruts. He stopped to remove a stone from one of his sandals. His tunic clung to him damply, and it already had an overlay of dirt.

Morgan felt a rush of tenderness; he was enduring this for her. She squeezed his arm, and he answered with a weak smile.

She thought of Elli, who had walked the same street. An ugly setting for her final scenes, yet she too had felt secure in Ai-won's love.

Such a fraud, she said to herself bitterly. All of Midia. Two *sorgots* in heavy mining costume passed them with averted eyes, and Morgan felt embarrassed to be a gawking tourist in her silks.

The man at the office was apologetic. "If you had called from Ferrano, we would have met you there. Such an uncomfortable trip in a small flitter. We don't get many visitors, so I'm afraid we are not well prepared. But I have arranged a special tour. This pipe we are working now has just been opened, and you may even see some rough diamonds being taken out. I think you will find it interesting."

"Will it be dangerous?" In spite of the heat, Oo-lors was pale.

"No, no. We would not expose you to anything hazardous. There will be no blasting."

They were issued helmets and coveralls and boots. Their guide arrived—a mine supervisor named A-kal. He was muscular, for a Midian, and he did not smile. "I have an airsled to take you to the mine," he said. "But before we start, I must have it understood that I am to be completely in charge. When we go underground, you must follow me closely and do exactly what I say."

"Of course." Oo-lors gulped nervously.

Once more Morgan assured him that he need not come with her, and again he refused to remain behind.

Winds buffeted them during the short hop to the mine. A-kal concentrated on his piloting and did not speak, and Oo-lors sat white-knuckled. Morgan was too concerned with Oo-lors's increasing anxiety to worry herself about possible hazard. After all, they had been guaranteed safety. The *aliti*, she thought, was simply unable to accomodate himself to conditions he had never known.

They landed near the bottom of the gorge. An assortment of ramshackle buildings looked temporary, hastily erected. The only sturdy one, a fused prefab, sheltered behind a bank of rock rubble. It contained A-kal's office.

He offered them coffee, which they refused. "Then let us get on with the tour," he said. "We will begin with the sorting sheds."

Inside one of the rickety structures *sorgots* worked the grease tables and the enormous vibrating pans. A-kal provided a commentary, competing with the din of the machinery, but Morgan missed most of it.

Outside, the supervisor hurried them on to the mine, a gaping black pit that he explained was the mouth of a primeval volcano. At the pithouse he adjusted their helmet lights and fitted them with airpacs and nose masks.

"Isn't the mine ventilated?" Morgan asked.

"It is not necessary," A-kal replied. "The miners are accustomed to the atmosphere, but it would be uncomfortable for you." He motioned them forward, and they descended on a creaking elevator, a thousand stomach-churning meters into the earth. Morgan gripped a stayrope, as did Oo-lors, but their guide balanced himself with ease. "This pipe is a most promising one," he said. "We hit *ferklith* early, and it is a rich vein." The elevator slowed, shook alarmingly, and stopped, and they stepped out onto a platform that extended into a cavernous horizontal shaft.

A-kal pulled them out of the way as a car loaded with black rock rumbled toward them. *Sorgot* miners, half naked and glistening with sweat, rode it onto the elevator and disappeared above. Morgan felt a ringing in her ears. The air was heavy and hot against her face, and even with her breather she knew a moment of suffocating panic.

"We have been working this shaft for six months now." A-kal's voice seemed to come from far away. Morgan wiped her face and breathed deeply. She tried to concentrate on something not connected with the mine—the wind in her face as she had felt it gliding over the south coast—and it worked. Her senses cleared, and the voice of the guide issued distinctly again. "The blasting has been completed, and the men are now removing the loosened *ferklith*. We would be a hindrance to them here, so we will go deeper and examine a new shaft where work has not yet started."

The elevator returned, and they went farther down. Under his helmet light Oo-lors's face was ashen. Morgan took his hand and received a faint answering pressure. She would have plenty to say to Alison, she thought, about the pick-and-shovel conditions. With all the wealth of Midia. . .

They were at the lowest level, except for their headlamps dark as a Stygian pit. A-kal shone a miner's lamp at the walls of the shaft. Between the braces the *ferklith* gleamed dull black. "Could there be diamonds in there?" Morgan asked. "Could I actually see them?"

"We will go in a short distance, and you may find something," A-kal said. "As I explained, this shaft has not yet been worked." He placed himself between Morgan and Oo-lors. "You go first," he said to Morgan. "This way I can watch out for both of you."

Morgan walked cautiously into the dark tunnel. *Ferklith* rubble covered the floor, and as she advanced the rocks became larger and heaped in scattered piles. She stopped before a chest-high mound that partially blocked her progress.

"Go on through," A-kal shouted. "I will be with you in a moment."

She was almost around the rock pile when an odd sound, like a scuffle, caused her to stop and look back. Two long shapes struggled, the flickering lights of their headlamps casting lurid dancing shadows.

"Oo-lors!" Morgan screamed and ran toward him, just as the rocks exploded behind her.

She came to consciousness on a stretcher. Oo-lors's face swam in the blur of pain that centered on her right arm. He spoke in Midian to the doctor, and even in her agony she could tell how frightened he was.

A needle in her other arm eased her, and she drifted in and out of clouds during a series of transfers and surgical procedures that ended finally in an antiseptic hospital room.

The clouds dissipated. She was in a webbed bed, the burns on her body covered with skingel. Her right shoulder and half of her right arm were bandaged. The rest of her arm was missing.

"Do you know who you are?" a nurse asked. "Tell me your name."

Morgan did so.

"Can you count to ten? Do you know what month it is?"

Morgan successfully established her mental acuity. "But my arm . . . where am I?"

"The patient is fully conscious," the nurse said into the vocom.

A man came into the room. "Please. Don't be alarmed. You'll be placed in a regeneration tank as soon as your tissues begin to heal." He was a Terran, a distinguished elder-stateman type. Morgan looked again and recognized the Terran ambassador.

The accident came back to her. "What happened in the mine?" she asked. "All I remember is the rocks blowing up."

"*Ferklith* is extremely unstable," he said. "Still, it should not have exploded spontaneously. The mine manager claims it did, but I wonder. . . . Have you done anything here that might cause you to have enemies?"

Morgan's breath caught in her throat. It had been a setup, she knew now with certainty. The entire trip.

But if she told him, if there was an official investigation, it would be the end of her career and finis to the *sorgot* cause. The Terran worlds were firmly committed to noninterference, and no matter how he felt privately the ambassador could never condone her actions.

She swallowed her anger and shook her head. "No, I can't imagine any reason."

The ambassador patted her left hand. "Then, you are not to worry about anything. Midian Mining is distressed about the accident, and will pick up the tab for the regeneration. It'll be a long process, you know—three or four months."

Morgan sighed. "I'm due for a long rest."

She floated in a warm liquid, only her head and her left hand outside the tank. Her body was weightless, and there was no pain in the slowly growing arm stump. She read and watched tridee and talked to visitors—Ah-nor and Ariane and Jallis and Firkin.

Oo-lors did not come. He had gone on tour with clients, Ah-nor said; to the subcontinent and beyond. Morgan was relieved. She did not know if she could have handled any more deceit.

Firkin told her of a government inspection at the school and an unexpected vacation. "We are to get completely new materials." The head mistress groaned and rolled her luminous eyes. "And imagine—we must now read each disk personally before we assign it. What a bother, and I cannot understand the purpose!"

Morgan had to get a message to Alison. A *sorgot* scrubwoman, attracted by her signals, took the scrawled note.

Alison came that evening, dressed as a gaudy tourist. In a strident voice she rambled on about Morgan's unfortunate accident and about the wonders of Trianka.

She bent over the tank as though listening to Morgan's response. "I know why you've sent for me," she whispered, "and you're not to worry. We know that the tampering was discovered, but no one knows who your accomplices were."

Morgan couldn't hide her distress. "But they'll

review all the disks now, and change them back. What we did will all be for nothing."

Alison smoothed Morgan's hair. "Not quite. They can't erase what's in the kids' heads. The seeds will grow.

"Can I get you any new bookspools?" she said loudly to the vocom. "The latest Terran romances?" Then, in an undertone, to Morgan: "I'm sorry it ended so badly for you. Do you hate us for getting you involved?"

Morgan closed her eyes. "No, I don't even hate Oo-lors," she murmured. "Though he must have known what was happening during that whole trip to the mine."

She waited for Alison's I-told-you-so.

It did not come. She opened her eyes and challenged the older woman with her gaze. "Maybe he didn't know, until just at the end." She had gone over it so many times, the degree of his guilt, to no certain conclusion. She knew, however, that he wasn't the monster that Alison with her clamped lips obviously considered him. "I think he was really fighting against his conditioning," she insisted. "He actually saved my life, you know. Maybe you're right about the seeds."

"I know I am." The mouth relaxed. "Come back in ten years and see."

"I'd like to. Maybe I will." Morgan felt the beginnings of a smile, the first time she had experienced the slightest optimism since her injury.

"By the way, you're looking very well," Alison said. "Did you know that besides a new arm there are residual benefits to spending three months in that tank?"

"Oh? What do you mean?"

"It's almost the same as a rejuv treatment. Here, take a look at yourself." Alison held up a hand mirror.

Morgan saw a rosy face from which the familiar lines were beginning to fade. A face from her youth. She gasped. "My body, too?"

"Yes. Ask your doctor. Five years off for every month in the tank, I've heard."

The smile formed complete. The dial on her time clock would be reset, she thought, and there would be ample time for a new sort of adventure. Not a bad bonus, by any means.

"I think I'd like that coffee now," Morgan said. Talking about the Midian episode without revealing anything of her underground activities had been a strain. She wondered if Billingsgate suspected how much she had omitted.

He ordered the refreshments. "A pity it ended so badly," he said. "Most of our teachers come back from Midia with glowing reports." He stared at her tightly clasped hands. "It still distresses you, doesn't it?"

She made a conscious effort to relax. "No, not at all."

He raised his eyebrows.

"Well, maybe just a bit," she amended. "It was a shock, after all, nearly getting blown apart. What would you expect?"

"That you'd be ready to ask for an early retirement. Why didn't you?"

"I thought about it," she admitted. "But I had only four more years, and I wanted my full pension. So I took the Elyrian assignment, as a supervisor, and then I was home free."

Home, she thought. . . .

V. Earth

Morgan remembered the spaceport as being surrounded by desert. Now, the sprawling subdivi-
sions of Arizona City began at the gates. From
the ground taxi she could see nothing in any
direction but ramps and causeways and hard-
edged geometrical shapes; concrete and steel
obliterating every trace of cactus and sand.

As she peered through the windows she cradled her right elbow in her left hand, a habit of
the last four years. The regenerated arm was
fully functional, but slightly smaller than the
other.

"Been gone long?" the driver asked.

"Twenty years, my time. Sixty, yours." Morgan had been prepared for changes. Though she
had made the long jumps to her various posts
by hypership, there had been enough shorter
journeys through normal space to make time dila-
tion significant. She expected no adjustment
problems, however. She had already decided not
to look up old acquaintances, and she had no
family.

"Jeez, you musta gone out as a kid, then. One
of the colonies?"

"No, I'm a Space Corps teacher." She didn't
tell him about her rejuvenation on Midia. Let
him wonder.

Though forty-three, Morgan looked fifteen years

younger. She didn't mind having to retire. Her health was perfect, and besides the consultant fees she could still earn, she had well-invested savings to cushion her reentry into her homeworld. She was satisfied with the results of her career, though it wasn't the return she had envisioned when she had shipped out so long ago as a green probationer. There was no welcoming committee to meet her, no handsome spacer of a husband at her side, and only the memory of children—other people's children—whom she had known for too brief periods.

No matter, she thought. The first two girlish fantasies she could do without, and the last lack she would remedy soon enough.

The driver turned onto a controlled expressway and locked his vehicle into the grid. His hands free, he poured himself coffee. "Like some?" He turned to face Morgan. "Bet you're dying for real Earth grub. They all are. First thing they want, soon as they set their feet on good ol' Terra." He had a large, soft face, his expression complacent with the assumption that she would want to talk to him.

Morgan accepted a cup of the warmish black liquid. "What's the best local restaurant?" she asked. No point in disappointing him.

He told her, and pointed out whatever landmarks they could see beyond the lanes of speeding traffic. A flashing sign gave notice of an approaching exit. "You want the Space Academy, right? Know which section?"

"SEF." She showed him the address of the ed school annex.

"Sure. Next turnoff after this one." He punched the controls and the car moved into the appropriate lane. At the end of the offramp he reengaged manual drive and wove through congested streets until they came to a quiet buffer zone. Beyond it

Morgan could see the familiar domes and spires of the Academy.

A guard checked them through the gate and gave directions to faculty housing. Morgan's unit had a well-watered lawn and a glimpse of a pool. The driver regarded her with increased respect. "Let me guess: some guy's gonna be mighty glad to see you."

She halved his tip and carried in her duffel herself.

The apartment was small, but clean and cheerfully furnished. And it was hers for delivering only a couple of lectures a week.

Morgan unpacked in minutes, hanging up a barebones wardrobe and setting out her mementoes. A *kiri*-wood bowl from Parth. A Lurian filigree tray. Scrolls and paperweights and ornaments. Jewelry, mostly of sentimental value. A box of holos.

Twenty years on one coffee table.

No regrets, she told herself. It had been rewarding work and glorious adventure, but now it was time for a new chapter. Roots and nest building and a child of her own.

The apartment would do, for now. Later, when she had decided where to settle, she would have a bigger place, with perhaps a bit of land. She could afford it, for herself and the baby.

Suddenly impatient, she called the Med Center and set up an appointment. Unless the wheels of bureaucracy had been streamlined in recent years, which she doubted, it wasn't too soon to set them in motion. She knew what to expect; she had checked on Cygni. She would need a health certificate, a genetic search, a financial responsibility affidavit, and approval from half a dozen social agencies.

It would take a least three months, the lawyer had said. Morgan thought she could whittle it to two. She had no other claims on her time except for the lectures, which should be a snap. "The benefits of your experience for the new recruits," she had been told. Words of wisdom from an old warhorse.

The directors would get a surprise when they saw her, she thought with a smile. And why not get those formalities over with, too? She changed into a fresh jumpsuit and set off for the administration offices.

The air was hotter than she remembered, the sky tainted with a bluish haze from the city center. She checked the underground transport map, but decided to walk. Earnest students passed her, hurrying, swinging their green cases. At the plaza fountain, crowds still milled; heavy discussions and light flirtations. A young woman with red hair perched on the bronze knee of Osterwold's statue, dangling her feet in the water.

It had been Morgan's favorite leisure spot. She listened to fragments of conversation. "Adamson was tough today. And why do we need to know those formulas, anyway?" "Can you believe the ground racer his old man gave him? Just for passing first comps." "He thinks I'm repressed. I'll show him, this weekend."

She had been no different. Unhearing and oblivious to what she was getting into. They would listen politely to her lectures, she knew, but her words would not register. They would go out to unimaginable worlds as naive as she had been.

The gulf stretched huge as the weight of more than sixty years seemed to settle on Morgan. She could still get out of her obligations here, and she considered it.

"Morgan! Morgan Farraday!"

She started, and looked around. A security guard ran toward her, waving frantically.

What regulation had she broken? she worried as she groped for her ID.

He came closer, and she gasped. The man's hair was more gray now than blond, and the imposing physique was slightly thicker in the midsection, but Morgan had do difficulty recognizing Arnie Vernor.

"What are you . . ."

"I never expected . . ."

"You look . . ."

They both spoke at once, stopped, laughed, and embraced.

"You first," Arnie said. "Ten—no, eleven years. Looking at you, I can't believe it. Where did you go, after Hedron II? And how long have you been here? God, I can't believe it!"

Morgan laughed again. "I can't either. I didn't expect to see anyone I knew. I just got here. I was on Elyria for four years, and before that on Midia. When I left Hedron I stayed on the stations for a while, and then I did a stint on Beta Hydri I. Ugh, what a world! Now I'm out to pasture, so to speak. I'm here at SEF as a consultant for the Corps. Faculty status and all the perks, but I was just wondering if I'll fit in anymore."

"I know what you mean." Arnie glanced self-consciously at his guard's uniform.

It had no insignia, Morgan saw. He must have retired, too, and taken a civilian job. "Now tell me about yourself," she said. "I gather you're out of the Space Force."

He grimaced. "General Cross saw to that."

"But . . . you were his fair-haired boy, on Hedron II."

"That was before I relieved him of his wife."

"You and Miranda! You're married?"

"We were. For three years. She's got someone else, now." He held up a hand. "But no sympathy, please. It's good riddance, as far as I'm concerned. And I've got the kids."

Morgan gaped. "How many?"

"Two. Twins, a boy and a girl. I've got pictures, but ..." He checked his watch. "Look, I can't talk to you any longer now, much as I'd like to. It's time for my hourly patrol. If I don't clock in at the main gate, I'll be chewed out for loafing." He compressed his lips. "It's a crummy job, but I need it."

He took her hand. "Can you see me tonight? I'd like you to meet Danny and Dee."

Morgan's head was swimming. "Tomorrow would be better. I just got off the shuttle, and I'm due to collapse in a couple of hours." She handed him her card. "Here's my address. Come over for dinner, you and the children."

"*I* was going to invite *you*."

"Next time." They both grinned. Arnie took off at a fast lope, but stopped to wave before he rounded the corner of the plaza.

As Morgan finished her walk to the administration building, she no longer thought of escaping from her commitments. Arnie Vernor, after all these years, she mused.

Delila and Daniel were shy eight-year-olds. Both were blond and blue-eyed, but apart from that they were not identical. Danny was thin and fine-featured, a high-strung child who found it difficult to sit still. Dee was stocky and placid, not at all pretty, though there was something appealing in her slow smile and whispery voice. Neither resembled Miranda.

"Danny wants to be a space pilot," Arnie said by way of introduction, "and Dee is our zoologist. She's crazy about anything with four legs or feathers."

Clued, Morgan had no difficulty getting Danny to talking, and finally managed to coax a few words from Dee. By dinner they were at ease with her. She served finger foods and a honey-laced dessert, all of which went over well. Afterward, when both children became sleepy, she put them down in her bed.

"They're sweet," she said to Arnie, serving coffee and brandy. "Good kids, both of them—I can tell. I was about their age when I lost my parents. Social took care of me, but it was never the same again. Dee and Danny are lucky to have you."

"I'm the lucky one," Arnie said. "Out of that fiasco of a marriage . . ."

"Yes, I'm curious about that." She regarded him with mock severity. "You really had me fooled. All that time on Hedron II you were juggling the two of us?"

"No, no," Arnie said quickly. A flush rose from his collar. "That is . . . well, not at first. I only started seeing Miranda after you turned me down. You hurt me, you know, and she was . . . available."

She let him off the hook. "I believe you. I also remember how avidly she was after you. But what went wrong? She must have been pretty desperately in love, to leave the general."

"Maybe she was, at first. But there was a scandal, and the general gave me a bad review. I had to leave the service. Miranda missed her status—she couldn't adjust to being the wife of a common civilian. Then, when she produced two babies, it was the proverbial straw.

"The embarrassment," he explained when Morgan looked puzzled. "She actually wanted to place one of the twins with Social. It was the beginning of my . . . disenchantment."

"Then the breakup was your idea?"

"No, I would have stuck with her. She left us when the twins were a year old. A retired banker.

"She hasn't been to see them in four years." He gave Morgan a strained smile. "And you: you've never married?"

"No, you were the closest I came. Somehow, it

never seemed to fit into my wandering life."
She filled him in on her most recent adventures,
including an edited version of the disaster on
Midia.

"Those Midians were responsible for this," she
said, stretching out her arms so he could see the
difference.

Arnie whistled softly. "What happened? I've
never seen an imperfect regenerated limb before."

"I can only guess. I wasn't popular with the
establishment on Midia. The doctors pretended
to be mystified, but I think they knew. A final
slap at a troublesome meddler."

"Diluting the fluid in the tank?"

"Just for the last week, it would have stopped
the growth enough to leave me with this going-
away present."

"It isn't really noticeable," Arnie said. "It could
have been worse."

"I know. And what they gave me, inadver-
tently, more than makes up."

He raised his eyebrows.

"I went to the Med Center today. Obstetics.
For all my years, I got an S-1 rating. I've filed
for permission, and as soon as my clearance
comes through I'll have a child, too."

Mixed emotions warred on his face. "That's
wonderful, Morgan, but ... it's tough, raising
kids alone. Or ... did you have someone in
mind?"

"No, nothing like that. I'm going to the sperm
bank. And I'm pretty well fixed financially. I
won't have any problems providing for one
child." She took his hands. "Arnie, be happy for
me. I've thought about it for so long."

He still looked less than pleased. "I had hoped,
back on Hedron, that you and I . . ."

"I know," she said, stopping him. "But it
worked out for the best, didn't it? You have
Danny and Dee, and now I can have my baby,

too. And who needs all the aggravation of a spouse and a marriage contract? Look at your experience."

"If you put it that way ..." He managed to unknot his brow, "I *do* wish you well, Morgan. You'll make a great parent. I always thought so."

"I'm going to depend on you, for help and hand-holding. You're the only friend I have on this planet."

"You can count on it." He locked his fingers into hers, but a noise from the bedroom caused him to release them abruptly.

Danny stood in the doorway, blinking his eyes and whimpering. "I had to ... I didn't know where ..." He pulled at his wet pajama legs in an agony of embarrassment.

Arnie went to him. "It's okay, sport. We'll fix you up." He led him to the bathroom.

When they returned, Danny was dressed in his day clothes. "We ought to be going, anyway," Arnie said. "Danny, go wake up your sister." He handed the boy a sweater. "She can put this on over her jamies.

"I hope he didn't ruin your bed," Arnie whispered when Danny was gone. "He has this problem, but I didn't expect, for such a short time..."

"Arnie, I think I still love you," Morgan said, surprising them both.

Even stripping the bed could not lower Morgan's spirits. Everything at last was going her way. Not that finding Arnie again would change her plans—he had his life and she had hers—but it was an inestimable comfort not to be alone.

She waxed indignant for Arnie, thinking of his lot. After his years of service—from security chief of an entire station to an ordinary guard! He should have had commendations and a decent pension, instead of disgrace and scrabbling to support a motherless family.

She wouldn't have expected any better of Miranda, Morgan thought, but it was a shame for Arnie to have been so taken. And she was partially to blame, leaving him wounded and susceptible while she had gone blithely off to another assignment.

She would make it up to him, she vowed, smiling dreamily at certain recollections. She hugged herself. Marvelous, to have such a second chance!

However, Morgan found that Arnie's juggling of work and domestic duties left him little time for himself. She met him briefly, for after-work drinks, but he had to hurry home to the children. She came for the promised dinner, to a shabby apartment in a block of low-rent units within sight and sound of the expressway. She brought gifts for each child: a book of starmaps for Danny and a birdwatcher's guide for Dee.

Danny clutched his present and retreated into a corner, where he pored over it eagerly.

Dee studied the pictures in hers, then appealed in turn to Arnie and to Morgan. "What's this one?" "What's the name of this bird?"

Arnie, busy chopping and stirring, gave the child quick answers. Morgan pointed to the text and sounded out the letters. "You try," she said, assisting Dee as she stumbled along. The child was willing to learn, Morgan saw, but she needed an intensive course of personal coaching.

"What kind of a school do they attend?" she asked Arnie, in the kitchen.

"Arizona City P.S. 104," he said. "Sixty in one third-grade classroom. Five teachers and God knows how many aides, and Dee still can't read worth a damn. I know she's bright enough, but. . ."

"I could teach her," Morgan said. "She mustn't be allowed to fall behind. If I could spend an hour a day with her . . ."

"You'd do that?"

"Gladly. I'm committed to giving two classes a week at the ed school, but other than that my time's my own.

"And yours, if you want it," she added. To hell with being coy.

Arnie turned from the stove with a look Morgan remembered well. She was ready to be kissed when Danny burst into the kitchen. "Will you see if the table's all right?" he said to his father. "We can't remember where the spoons go."

"I'll come look," Morgan said. She flashed a grin at Arnie.

She found Dee fussing with the pieces of flatware, her face puckered in concentration.

"I think . . . here," Morgan said, placing the spoon. "Does that look right?"

Dee nodded solemnly and corrected the other place settings. "It's hard for me to remember, too," Morgan said. "Especially when I've lived on so many worlds. There are eating customs so different from ours that you wouldn't believe it."

"Tell us," both children chorused.

Morgan was well into her travelogue when Arnie brought in the food. "I'm going to see some of those places," Danny said when the conversation was resumed.

Morgan smiled. "You mean when you're a hotshot pilot?"

"No, before that. We're all going to another planet to live. A better place than this, with grass and trees all over and lots of animals for Dee and maybe not any streets at all." He shuddered at the intermittent rumbles that came from the direction of the expressway.

"Animals," Dee echoed, with shining eyes.

"Is that true?" Morgan asked, though one glance at Arnie's face provided her answer.

"I was going to tell you tonight," he said, his

initial embarrassment supplanted by a look of
entreaty. "Please don't be angry. I had my reasons for not wanting to spring it on you right
away."

I'll bet you did, Morgan thought. Disappointment flooded her, but she maintained her com-
posure for the sake of the children. "So which
colony is it to be?"

Arnie relaxed slightly. "I've applied to several. They're all primitive, with one or more
hardship factors. We can't afford the premium
colonies, and anyway, I wanted a newly opened
one."

"I see. Will you be leaving soon?"

Again he gave her a pleading look. "I don't
know yet. I'm still waiting to hear if we've been
accepted."

"Why don't you go, too?" Danny cried. He
bounced up and down in his chair. "They'd be
sure to take you, you know so much about all the
different planets."

Arnie shook his head at the boy, but said
nothing.

"I just got here," Morgan said. "It's home, for
me. I'm not about to go out again."

Danny subsided. "Oh. Well, we don't like living where there are so many people. We want
our own house, and Daddy will have a better
job when he learns how to be a farmer."

Morgan turned to Arnie. "Are you being trained?"

"You bet. Agriculture and mining and carpen-
try and even a little basic medicine. A regular
jack-of-all-trades."

"You'll be selected, then." Her voice was dry.

Danny continued to chatter, filling up awkward silences. After dinner the males cleared
while Dee showed Morgan her current menag-
erie: an ant farm, a white mouse in a cage, and a
rock lizard that made its home in a box under

her bed. "They're a secret," she confided. "If the manager finds out, we'll have to move."

Dee's complexion had the pastiness of too much indoor living. Her own daughter, Morgan promised herself, would be reared where there were parks. She would have a cat and a dog, and perhaps even access to a pony.

Arnie, however, had to live where there was work. She couldn't blame him for his decision to emigrate. Only for allowing her to resurrect old feelings.

"I'm sorry," he said when they were alone. They sat far apart on a lumpy sofa that had once been form-shaping. "I was afraid to tell you before. I thought you might not want to see me, might not want to get to know the children. I didn't want to lose you a second time."

"But you will, when you go away. What would be the point of . . . starting something now?"

"Things may change."

She resisted the appeal in his eyes. "For you or for me? I'll admit I entertained some fantasies of a combined family, here, but I meant what I said to Danny. No way am I leaving Earth again."

He stared at the floor between his feet. "That's it, then. I'm committed to go, if they'll have me."

She stood up to leave. "I'll honor my promise to help Dee."

"You needn't."

Anger surfaced. "Let me decide that! It has nothing at all to do with you." She stood ramrod-straight and glared.

He rose, too. "Are you sure about that?"

Strong arms picked her up and swung her while she kicked. "Arnie Vernor, put me down! I remember your tricks!" His lips found hers while he lowered her to the sofa.

Much later, when she left, there was no more

bitterness. Nothing had been resolved between them, but Morgan was determined to live in the present as far as Arnie was concerned. He needed her more than she did him, so she wasn't unduly worried about being lured away from her blueprinted future—a future that definitely did not include any more primitive planets.

Her work at the Academy was about as she had expected: half of her students were apathetic and the other half chafed to reshape the galaxy according to their own lights. She presented her holos of cannibalistic aliens and colonists wearing animal skins, stressed the Corps doctrine of cultural noninterference but suspected that her words made little impression.

Far more satisfying were her tutoring sessions with Dee. The child made steady progress to grade-level reading as the daily hour stretched more often to two. On a weekend when Arnie was working, Morgan took both children to the nearest parklands. The twins ran ecstatically over sand and scrubby grass, but Morgan was disappointed by the admitting lines and the fences and the constant electronic surveillance.

Her own program slowly took shape as one after another government agency examined her and pronounced her fit to be a parent. She began to visit real estate offices, where she discovered that her savings would purchase less than she had expected. She flew to northwestern Canada, to look at lots she could afford. She had had visions of forests, but the land was all cleared and graded, and the megalopolis of Cariboo City reached its concrete fingers to the edges of the development. There were parklands beyond, however, and she would have bought except for fear of the winters. She finally gave up thoughts of land and made a down payment on a floating condo unit on the Gulf of California.

She visited the sperm bank and listed her specifications.

Morgan was at Arnie's place, waiting for Dee to come home for her lesson, when she told him.

The big man reddened and then turned coldly pale. "You'd prefer an anonymous donor to me? Would it be so terrible to have our child?" Hurt pride spoke in every rigid line of his body.

She had guessed how he would react, but she had told him for a reason. In spite of everything she said to the contrary, she knew that Arnie still harbored hopes that she would do an about-face and exchange her future for his. He and the children had been accepted for Prantax Primus, and the ties had to be cut.

"No, it wouldn't be terrible at all," she said. "It's just that . . . it would make it that much harder for me to see you leave.

"And I will *not* change my mind. I've read up on Primus, and it's no place I'd ever want to live. An iceball on one side and a desert on the other. The settlers on Prantax Beta want it colonized by friendlies, so they're willing to subsidize a transport from Earth, but I notice none of them are volunteering. And that's where you want to take the children."

"There are habitable zones at the poles. Though of course it won't be anything like your floating resort."

"I've earned it, Arnie."

His mouth twisted. "Of course you have." Bitterly. "So when do you get . . . injected?"

"Next week." He would get over it, she knew, but she didn't need to stay and be made to feel guilty. "Tell Dee I'm sorry, I'll see her tomorrow." She collapsed her portable reader and threw it and the bookspools into their case, snapping it shut.

She glanced at her watch. "Aren't the children late?"

Arnie confirmed it. "Half an hour." A deeper line appeared on his brow. "God, they know to come right home. . . ."

Morgan sat down again.

In ten minutes the phone rang in the kitchen. Arnie was gone for much too long. When he reported, his face was gray. "It's Dee. She and Danny were playing on the pedway overpass, coming home from school, and she fell off. She's at City General."

They took a helicab to the hospital roof, but then got lost inside, in the sprawling corridors. When they finally located Dee, they were not allowed to see her.

A nurse directed them to a waiting room. "She's in diagnostic. We'll let you know as soon as there's a report."

Arnie would not be put off. "But—how badly is she hurt? How was she, when they brought her in?"

"She was unconscious. I'm sorry, I can't tell you any more."

Danny sat huddled on a corner chair, his tear-streaked face white with fear.

Morgan took him into her arms. "We were playing tag," he sobbed, "and she climbed up to get away."

"You couldn't help it," Morgan said. "The doctors here are good. They'll know what to do."

They waited in the bare-walled room as time crawled.

A doctor appeared in the doorway. "Are you the parents?"

Arnie got up, while Morgan clutched Danny and forgot to breathe. She heard terrifying fragments: "Fractures . . . her skull . . . bleeding . . ." She released Danny and walked on wooden legs to stand beside Arnie.

"The broken bones are no problem, and there are no internal injuries. But her brain . . ." The doctor displayed a colored scanprint. "We can keep her alive, but in my opinion it would be best to . . ."

Arnie had the glazed look of a man in shock.

"No!" Morgan shouted.

The doctor regarded her with compassion. "I know how you must feel, but here—look at this. You can see the clots, and there, the bone fragments."

It looked bad, but Morgan knew from her own experience that miracles could be accomplished if one had the means. "Can't you operate?" she asked.

He hesitated. "In my opinion, it would be useless. It would be a life-risking procedure, even with microlaser techniques. Possible blindness. Paralysis. And in any case, for even a chance of successful recovery there would have to be braintissue reconstruction. It's a new field, and we've no one on staff who could do it." He spread his hands, apologetic. "A public hospital, you know. . ."

"Who's the nearest qualified neurosurgeon?" Arnie asked.

Morgan corrected him. "No, the best one anywhere."

The man looked from one to the other. "That would be Jonas Oswandu, in South Africa. But his fees are—"

"Never mind that," Morgan said. "Get him."

"We would have to move the patient to a hospital with the proper facilities."

"Which do you recommend?"

"Zion Memorial, in Dallas. But it's a private hospital—"

"Stop carping about money," Morgan snapped. "I can pay whatever it costs. Just make the arrangements."

The doctor finally believed her. He spoke rapidly into a vocom, and she and Arnie and Danny were led off in opposite directions: Arnie to view Dee through a glass wall, Danny to a cafeteria with a friendly nurse, and Morgan to a banklike financial office where she signed voucher after voucher to ensure that Dee would have the finest care.

Morgan collected Danny and waited some more, this time in a pleasantly decorated lounge. Arnie came in, looking better. "Dr. Oswandu is on his way by priority tachjet. Morgan, I don't know how to . . ."

"Then don't, please. I'm not even thinking about that, now."

He looked even more relieved. "They're moving Dee now, and I'm going with her. Do you suppose you could keep Danny for a few days?"

"Of course."

"Will Dee be all right?" the boy asked.

Arnie hugged him. "We hope so. We're doing all we can."

At home, with Danny, Morgan cooked food neither of them touched, went for a walk, and played mindless holo games. They both skirted their consuming worry. When it was dark she put the child to bed—this time with a protective sheet—and gave up the pretense of normalcy. She sat numbly and stared at the phone.

It did not ring, though she kept vigil all night. In the morning she called the Dallas hospital and learned that Dee was in surgery.

She delivered Danny to his school and returned to sit by the phone some more.

She called at ten; the surgery was still in progress.

At one o'clock the call came from Arnie: Dee had withstood the operation well, and the doctors were hopeful. At three he called again: she had opened her eyes and spoken.

Morgan broke down and cried.

*   *   *

"So tell me everything you know about Prantax Primus," Morgan said. They were all—she and Danny and Arnie—sitting around Dee in her hospital bed. Dee's head was wrapped in a bubble of gauze. Her speech was slightly slurred and she had some blank spaces in her memory, but the doctors had assured them that it signified nothing serious. Dee would be able to leave Earth in the spring, as planned, with the colonial party.

"I thought you had looked it up," Arnie said. "I thought you were an expert on that planet."

"I only know the bad things," Morgan said. "Tell me its good points."

Danny jumped up from his chair. "It's always warm where we're going to be, and the days go on forever."

"That's right," Arnie said. "We can raise continuous crops."

"Sun-baked," Morgan muttered. "Synchronous rotation."

Arnie shook his head. "At the polar mountains it's quite temperate. There's an exchange of atmospheres from the light and dark sides, good soil and plenty of water."

"No trees," Morgan said.

"We'll build our houses of stone, so it'll be cool and dark inside whenever we want to escape from the sun."

"Big-planet gravity. One point three gees."

"Our muscles will adjust. We've already started on a program of exercising with weights—even Dee."

"Watch me!" The injured girl puffed out her cheeks as she grasped the handle of a suspended pulley with both plastic-encased arms and raised herself from the bed.

Morgan gasped and started to get up.

"It's okay." Arnie placed a hand on her arm. "Your high-priced therapist set up all those contraptions. Though in another week Dee won't need them; she'll be working out in the gym."

"I'll be s-stronger than anyone," Dee said. She managed a slow, slightly crooked smile.

Arnie's grip tightened as he looked from Dee to Morgan. "So what do you think now of your investment?"

"It's the best one I ever made." She meant it, feeling no regrets for her vanished soft and easy future.

Arnie was still troubled by his debt to her, Morgan knew, and she was about to absolve him from it. She hadn't told him yet, but she had missed her appointment at the sperm bank. And she had already started on her own exercise program.

It would be the first planet of Prantax for her too, for better or for worse.

"I was out of the Corps, and not teaching at all anymore," Morgan said. "Is there any need to go on?"

"I'm trying to see you as a total person, Farraday," Billingsgate said. "Everything is important." He fixed her with a gaze that made her feel more than ever like an insect under a microscope. *"Is there something you don't want to talk about?"*

"No, of course not," she lied. It was there anyway, in that inescapable file.

VI. Prantax Primus

Morgan had wandered far from camp when she first sensed the whisperer. She had left the rocky path that led up from the valley and was scrambling around the foothill boulders. The heat of Prantax beat fiercely upon her unprotected head, and she thought at first the odd sensation was a touch of sunstroke. There was no breeze, yet she felt the whisper of a caress upon her bare arms and legs. Someone—something—was watching her curiously, and the air was alive with unvoiced questions.

"What is it? Who are you?" she called, whirling to see in all directions. But the presence vanished as soon as she spoke. She saw nothing but the bare rocks around her, the jagged mountains ahead, and below, the narrow strip of green valley dotted with the tents of their compound.

It must have been the sun, she thought again, and replaced the hateful helmet. Arnie would fuss at her for not wearing it, but even perforated, it was a heat trap, making a sodden mess of her hair and sending rivulets of stinging sweat into her eyes. He would scold her, in any case, for leaving without telling him, but she had had to get away if only for a few hours from the regimented activity of the camp. And now she would have something to report, though she couldn't expect it to lighten Arnie's displeasure;

every new contact with the elusive whisperers only made him and the rest of the council more uneasy.

Morgan rested on a smooth boulder and gazed longingly at the airy spires she had hoped to reach. It seemed that somehow it must be cooler up there, and that she would be relieved of the burden of her weight. But it was impossible this shift. She had started too late, pushed herself too hard, and now exhaustion dragged at her leaden feet.

She descended slowly, finding the path and picking her way carefully over the loose stones. Though all of the colonists found exertion tiring, to Morgan, six months pregnant, it was doubly difficult. She stopped to rest once more, leaning on her pronged walking stick.

Again she felt the cool touch. A whispering sigh, like the soughing of a wind, came from the trail above. It urged her, wordlessly, to turn and retrace her steps.

She forgot her weariness as she followed the sound, her limbs curiously light. She was back to the boulders again before she heard the shouts of the search party.

"Mor-gan!" It was Arnie's voice. The unseen guide vanished and Morgan was once more solidly cumbersome, overheated and overtired, as she waited for her husband.

Red-faced and sweating, he struggled up the slope with an urgency that defied the gravity. His relief when he saw her quickly turned to exasperation. "Christ, honey, what do you think you're doing? We've a dozen men out looking for you, pulled off their workshifts. And you look like the beginnings of apoplexy." He began to swear again, as angry as she had expected.

It seemed that lately he could always make her feel a complete fool, and the worst of it was, this time he was right. She had no business

leaving without checking out, or being here at
all. But she clung to her pride and stubbornly
defended herself. "So I took a walk. Is that such
a crime? You needn't have come after me. It
isn't endshift yet and I haven't even left the
trail. What do you expect me to do—sit in that
stuffy tent hour after hour and twiddle my
thumbs? Even the littlest kids have their duties
but I'm not allowed to do anything useful."

"You know it's for your own good. The first
birth—we don't know what complications this
gravity will cause. And here you are, exerting
yourself, halfway up the mountain! It must be
your condition affecting your judgment. At least
that's the excuse I'll have to make for you."

He took her arm and helped her down the
path, his mouth a tight line. The other searchers, when they met them on the trail, did not
conceal their grumbles of annoyance. Morgan
felt so humiliated and so bone-weary that she
didn't mention then her contact with the ethereal aliens.

Arnie left her at the edge of the compound.
His anger was replaced by concern for her obvious fatigue. "I'm sorry I yelled," he apologized,
"but I was so worried." He kissed her lightly, as
if she might break from his touch. "Go home
and rest now. Promise? You know how important this baby is to all of us."

She nodded and managed a wavery smile.
Arnie loved her, she knew, even though these
days he tended to treat her more like a symbol
than a flesh-and-blood person. But then everyone did, for she and what she carried were the
assurance of their future.

Arnie's workshift was at the end of the valley,
at the city building site. A work party rumbled
by on a wagon filled with stones, and he caught a
ride with them.

Morgan watched it bump along the deeply

rutted road. The builders waved to workers in the fields and to an exploring party straggling down from the mountains. It was near endshift and everyone looked wilted, but the red-gold sun Prantax burned as always, a molten fire between the distant peaks. Low on the horizon, it dominated the landscape as it did the lives and thoughts of the colonists; it was the over-whelming fact of their world.

The colony had planted tenuous roots at the polar mountains, where a swollen river issued from the snows of darkside. They had divided their "days" into rotating eight-hour shifts: a workshift, a recshift, and a sleepshift, so a third of their number were always at labor. In four months grains had been planted and harvested, and a village of cool stone was arising which would eventually provide darkness when needed and relief from the constant sun.

For now, though, the only escape was in the shaded tents. Morgan headed for the one she shared with Arnie and the twins. Walking was easier on the packed clay of the compound area, but her legs still ached from the uphill climb. She ducked for a moment into the open mess tent and sank gratefully upon a bench.

Three harried workers were preparing the endshift meal. Plump, brown-eyed Lupe looked up from the stove. "God, Morgan, are you a welcome sight. Can you lend a hand? Shara didn't show up and we'll never be ready in time."

"Sure, I'll be glad to." She was halfway to her feet when Grant, the mess boss, motioned her back. He glared at Lupe.

"You know Morgan isn't supposed to work. If she even lifts a finger in here I may get in trouble with the council." He turned to Morgan. "Don't worry, we'll manage. Just sit there and keep out of the way."

He dumped an armload of plates on the table

and yelled at his two assistants to hurry it up. Lupe made a face behind his back, and Morgan answered with a shrug. She felt worse than useless, and left.

She paused outside the other big tent, the combined nursery and school. Piping voices drifted out, and she parted the doorflap and peered inside.

The smaller children occupied one corner, clapping and singing in a circle game. In the main section, two school-age groups seemed to be busy with writing lessons, copying from slides projected on the walls.

Morgan spotted Dee and Danny near the back. They were sitting on the floor, using their bench as a desktop while they scribbled and whispered and giggled. Dee's hair was grown to earlobe length. It was cut like Danny's, and with the weight she had lost the two were more like in appearance than they had ever been—at least as long as Morgan had known them.

Danny aimed a paper-wad bushwhacker at a boy in front of him. The victim jumped up with a gasp, and Beth McLean, one of the team teachers, came to investigate. Both twins assumed expressions of bland innocence.

Neither Beth nor Kai, the other teacher, had had previous classroom experience, and Morgan knew that she shouldn't be critical. Still, the horseplay and the wasted supplies . . . and they weren't even following the program that she had organized so carefully before she had been relieved.

Just because she had fainted one time. Morgan longed to go in and help out, but she knew better than to risk it. The twins would tell Arnie, and there would be another scene.

Besides, she was too tired. The ache moved from her legs to her back, and she lifted her stomach with both hands to ease it. Dr. Lin had made her a corset, but it was too hot to wear for long periods. Now, her bladder warned her that she had to get home quickly.

Half of the family tents were dark-shaded for rest or sleepshift, and the others were empty. Inside the Vernors' it was stuffy, as usual. Morgan did not open the vent flaps, however; the dim light was soothing to her sun-seared eyes. She used the toilet and then lowered herself to a cot and stretched out, surrendering to the pull of the earth.

Heavy . . . she was so heavy. The walls of the tent closed in on her as outside the mountains enclosed their valley, and she lay there trapped— by her body and by the colony and by the huge perverse planet.

She had lost her identity and become a monument to fertility: a breeding machine to ensure the continuance of the species on a bleak outpost that would never be home to her. It was too much to bear. She thought of Beth, who had the job that should have been hers. She thought of flighty Shara, who could miss an entire workshift and yet not have a search party out after her. She thought of the whisperer on the mountain who had no body at all. Lighter than air, free and floating. She thought of her child, the colony's child, red and squalling and chained to the earth. In her fancy it became a whisper child, dancing light as gossamer on the mountain peaks.

She knew she had had too much sun.

Arnie agreed, when she told him at dinner about the whisperer. He had left the twins at the mess tent and brought a tray for her. He was still vexed. "Heat exhaustion," he said. "Sunstroke. I'll have Doc check you over before sleepshift, and from now on you're not to leave the tent unless you've someone with you. I simply can't trust you anymore." He watched gimlet-eyed to see that she ate every morsel on her plate. "Unfortunately," he continued, "we'll have to make a report, and I'll get hell for letting you wander away like that."

She bridled. "You're not my keeper. And I know it was a real contact. It felt exactly the way the others described them. Captain Hudson and those yes-men of his on the council just won't admit that there's something here they can't explain."

Arnie frowned, but Morgan rushed on. "Yes, I mean you, too—you know you always go along with everything he says. And furthermore, I'll be damned if I'll spend the next three months cooped up in this sweatbox."

To reinforce her ultimatum she pushed aside her plate. "I've had enough to eat." Then, unaccountably, she ruined the effect of her revolt by bursting into tears.

"Please don't," Arnie begged, holding her. His tough veneer cracked, and he was as tender as he had been in the days before the rigors of survival had buried gentler attitudes. "It's just that I can't bear the thought of losing you. Without you none of this—the waiting, the work and the struggles—none of it would be worthwhile. You know that, don't you?"

"I thought it was just the baby you were concerned about." She was only half teasing.

"How can you say such a thing?" He pressed his face against her stomach. She could feel him tremble.

She brushed at the stubborn cowlick that would never lie flat with the rest of his neatly cropped hair. It made him seem childlike, for all his show of macho pioneer courage. Dear Arnie, she thought, who had placed all of his hopes in this venture. Their futures and the children's futures. He was building a spacious house for them—the house of his dreams—with views of both the river and the mountains. He would never feel fettered as she did here, for his muscular frame had adapted easily to the gravity.

Morgan didn't think she ever would. She shifted to a more comfortable position, cradling her right arm.

Arnie reached up and rubbed it. "Does it bother you?"

"No, not—" She checked herself. She had been about to say "not any more than everything does, here." Arnie would never know that to her their new world was not a glorious challenge but a prison.

He whispered, "Promise you'll never leave me."

"I do; I promise," she said, stroking his head.

Dr. Lin came, a slender white-haired woman with kind eyes and gentle hands. She examined Morgan and reassured them both. "Everything's normal," she said. "I don't predict any problems."

The twins returned from after-dinner play. "Daddy, can we go swimming?" Danny begged.

"Please, Daddy, it's so hot. We'll never get to sleep unless we cool off." Dee pulled on his arm. Both children were strong and brown from hours outdoors.

Arnie agreed. They didn't ask Morgan to join them, and it hurt her, even though she wouldn't have gone. The river had a single calm stretch, but it was at the end of the valley near the houses. Too far for her to walk.

She made do with a sponge bath, prepared the cots, and hung up the curtain that provided privacy for her and Arnie. Not that they needed it—their sweaty grapplings had all but stopped, in spite of Cleo Lin's assurances that it was safe enough.

Morgan spent a wakeful sleepshift wondering at her temerity in creating an innocent hostage to an uncertain fate. If she had known what she

would find here she would never have considered it, but the baby had been conceived before
they left Earth. The other women had been wiser,
and they still waited to see whether Morgan
would deliver safely.

It was the least of her fears. Far worse, bur-
dened as she was with another life, were the
unrelenting sun and the heavy pull of the earth;
the bodiless phantoms who whispered.

Perhaps Arnie was afraid sometimes, too, but
he never let on, following the example of their
captain. Morgan and Arnie went together to report her experience at firstshift council in the
captain's tent, and Hudson reacted with predict-
able impatience.

"Not another one!" Captain Hudson had a
bristly mustache over a thin-lipped mouth. He
stood militarily erect. "I've had it up to here
with these phony reports. That fool Chandru
and his 'psychic touches'—he started it! Hysteria, that's all it is. Communicable hysteria, and
each of these so-called 'contacts' is adding fuel
to it." He turned to the others in the tent. "We
all know there's nothing out there. The Betans
explored the area several times, and our own
probes showed no sentient life readings on the
entire planet. We wouldn't be here, otherwise.
Until somebody *sees* something, there's nothing
I can do. We all have more serious problems to
be concerned about."

He focused on Arnie. "What was she doing
away from camp, anyway? Can't you keep her
home, in her condition?"

Arnie said nothing.

"And now it's Shara who's missing," Hudson
continued, his voice rising again. "Probably out
looking for those mysterious ghosts you people
insist on imagining. Morgan, go on home and
stay there. The rest of you, get search parties
organized. Another workshift shot to hell!"

Morgan hastily left the tent, but lingered at the door until Arnie and the other council members filed out. "Shara has been gone for two shifts," she said, pulling Arnie into the shade of the overhang. "She didn't show up for her mess duty."

"I know," Arnie said. "It looks bad. We're going to drag the river."

"Try the mountain, where I was," Morgan said. "But keep going higher—up to the crags."

"Do you know something?"

"No, it's just a feeling. Captain Hudson would say it's nonsense, but look up there anyway."

Morgan spent two restless hours inside the tent. The twins left for recshift with the duty sitters, and she worked on records, the only activity she was allowed. It was difficult to concentrate, however. She looked up in relief when Lupe stopped by.

"Any news?"

Lupe shook her head. Her shoulders drooped. "Morgan, I feel terrible about this. I should have told Hudson right away that Shara was missing, but I kept thinking she'd show up any minute. I figured she was out behind a rock somewhere with someone—you know how she is. But no one's seen her for sixteen hours!" Her words ended in a wail.

"Don't blame yourself," Morgan said. "Grant could have said something, too—he was in charge. He probably thought the same thing as you and didn't want to spoil his own chances by reporting her. I've seen the way he's been eyeing her."

They were both silent, thinking of the vibrant, pleasure-loving young woman.

"Well, I'd better get back to the search," Lupe said. "The whole shift's out looking. They're even using the airsled."

Everyone but me, Morgan thought bitterly.

She dragged a stool to the doorway and sat spraddle-legged, her hands resting on the mound of her stomach. The camp and surrounding fields were deserted and eerily quiet. Beyond the low rise of the foothills the mountains cut darkly across the bright sky.

The baby kicked and Morgan sat absorbed. She felt the other touch first on her hands; then, when she moved them, the gentlest of pressures on her stomach. The whisper swirled around her ears and danced off. It seemed to offer freedom and a lightness too tempting to resist. Without thinking she got to her feet and followed.

She was almost to the mountain road when she came to her senses. Her visitor was gone and an airsled circled in low over the fields. She watched as they unloaded a stretcher.

Shara's broken body had been found well into the heights, at the foot of a sheer cliff.

Morgan thought of Dee and Danny, on recshift. What if they had gone hiking? She hurried back to the compound, where she found them safe on the playing field.

For now, that is. Were any of them safe any longer? she wondered.

Lupe ran up to her, breathless. "Captain Hudson wants you. Another council meeting, right away."

The captain appeared shaken. "How did you know where we'd find Shara?" he asked. "Arnie told me you suggested where to look."

"It was the whisperer, and I've felt it again," Morgan said. "Chandru is the only one who would understand. Let me talk to him."

"Get him," Hudson ordered, "and round up everyone else who's reported a contact. Maybe I've been wrong to dismiss this so lightly."

The captain paced and chewed on an unlit pipe until they were gathered. In a total about-face he listened with close attention to Morgan and the others as they recounted their experiences, and was polite even to Chandru.

The young psychic couldn't resist one shot. "You recall I *did* warn you, just after we landed. I reported receiving definite vibrations, but not a one of you was concerned." He directed his gaze at the circle of sober-faced council members.

"Recriminations do no good now," Arnie said. "And after all, the area had been thoroughly probed."

"Pure mental energy wouldn't register," Chandru said. "But I'm not casting blame; I could have been more forceful, too. I wish . . ." His lips shaped a dreamy half-smile as his eyes seemed to focus on something far away.

"You wish what?" Morgan prompted.

Chandru came back to reality. "It's such an interesting phenomenon, I wish I'd had more chances to study it. Maybe I will, yet. But to anyone untrained, it's a definite threat."

"You keep saying 'it,' " Captain Hudson said. "Explain yourself. Just what are we faced with?"

"I don't know for sure. Some sort of force or entity that can exert a hypnotic influence. A potentially destructive one, if we take the worst possible interpretation of Shara's accident."

"Can you communicate with it—or them?" Hudson asked.

"Not in anything you can translate into words. What I've felt, and the others bear me out, was first a kind of curiosity, as if something was studying us. Not particularly dangerous. But now it's changed, to this strong summons Morgan described. Shara may have felt it; she was a sensitive, you know."

"You think it lured her to her death?"

"It's possible. No one in her right mind would be alone on those cliffs. We need a full meeting, Captain; everyone must be warned."

Hudson acted immediately. "Arnie, sound the

emergency siren. Cleo and Grant, roust out all
the sleepshifters. Direct everyone to the mess
tent. Let's move—fast!"

But it wasn't fast enough. Before the tent was
filled news came of two more disappearances.

One report was from the solar plant foreman:
"Hari Mallon. He just walked away from the work
crew. We were on our way to the site and he
headed off into the mountains like a bat out of
hell. Couldn't have caught up with him if I'd
tried."

Ruth from the lab had a similar report. "Kin
On. He was upset about Shara. We all were, so I
didn't notice at first when he didn't come back
from his break. I checked around, and someone
saw him on the mountain road, running faster
than anyone ever does in this gravity."

Both bodies were found below the cliffs.

"You know what those two had in common,
don't you?" Morgan said to the stunned council
members. They were in the front of the mess
tent, which was packed wall to wall, with the
overflow lined up outside.

She received only blank looks. Then Lupe
shouted from her spot atop one of the tables:
"Of course! They were Shara's lovers. Both of
them."

"The latest in a long line, if we can believe the
general gossip," Morgan said.

"It would seem that the lady is lonely," observed Chandru. An ominous quiet spread through
the tent as the import of his words was absorbed.

Captain Hudson paled. "You mean everyone
who has . . . had something to do with Shara
. . . is in danger?"

"I'm afraid so," Chandru said. "I'd better meet
right away with any of you who would be
affected and drill you in setting up mindblocks.
Otherwise . . ."

He didn't need to elaborate. A dozen visibly

shaken men, Captain Hudson among them, followed Chandru from the tent.

"There'll be some domestic rows later," Arnie whispered to Morgan.

"Are you sure you shouldn't join the parade?" she asked tartly.

Arnie refused to be amused. "Thank God I've never even been tempted." He squeezed her arm before returning to the business of the meeting. He and the remaining council members briefed everyone and set up a continuous guard system around the compound and at the work sites.

It worked, partially, though everyone, particularly the children, grumbled at the loss of freedom. Lupe succumbed to a whisperer when she was in the fields, but she was spotted and stopped before she reached the mountains. She remembered nothing but a dream of flight. Two more of Shara's lovers were summoned. Both were rescued, but one was found later, drowned, in a section of the river where no one swam. The worst blow, however, was when Chandru, who knew all about mindblocks, evaded the guards and followed a whisperer over the fatal cliffs. In the resultant confusion Janie Mallon, two years old, slipped away. She, too, was found too late.

Security doubled. The children were confined to their home tents or to the school. Everyone walked in pairs, even in the compound. The river was off limits, and the plain beyond the fields. The mountains, of course, were completely proscribed.

Morgan was no longer alone in her claustrophobic reaction. The delirious sense of adventure that they had all experienced in the first months vanished as the inhospitable desert and the frozen wastes of darkside shut them into a narrowing world.

Morgan hid her increasing fatalism as she did the whispers that now buzzed in her head like insects, clamoring and insistent. She was lost, she knew, if she followed them; and if she resisted, it would be worse. With each ounce she gained she was more sure that the earth of Primus would soon have her. She ate little, for all Arnie's and Dr. Lin's cajoling, yet she could scarcely support the growing weight of her stomach.

The tent became smaller each day as the children squabbled.

"I hate it in here; it's hot and there's nothing to do." Dee swept her arm across the top of the folding table, knocking the jumble of small stones and clay lumps to the floor.

"Hey, you can't do that! That was my city!" Danny left his makeshift hypership model and pounced on his sister with flailing fists.

"I can if I want to. It was mine, too." Dee yanked a handful of his hair.

Morgan separated them. "Danny's mean," Dee whined with an outthrust lower lip. "He won't let me play with his ships."

"Mean yourself. Crybaby."

"Stop it!" Morgan screamed. She shook Dee and gave Danny a sharp slap. Then, seeing the shocked expressions on both faces, she gave way to tears herself.

She couldn't handle it, she admitted silently. They would all be better off without her. She was no fit mother, no teacher, no good as a nursemaid, even. She didn't want to devise things for them to do; she only wanted to lie on her cot and not think at all.

Arnie continued to work as much as he could with all the restrictions, but finally even he had to admit that it was no longer a life. On a shift when the children were in school he hosted an unofficial meeting with Hudson and Cleo Lin and Tim McLean. Morgan served them coffee and then retired to her cot on the other side of the curtain. She could have stayed—Arnie and Dr. Lin both invited her—but Morgan wanted no part of the discussions. They could decide whatever they wanted; she knew that she would never escape the planet.

She lay weighted by the chains of her flesh and listened to meaningless words.

"If it were something we could fight," Tim said, "I'd say we should stick it out. But we have no weapons against these . . . whatever it is. We can't continue to live like this, in constant fear. Beth's paranoid already, and she's not the only one."

No one answered for several minutes. When Arnie did, his voice was bleak. "We've made such a good start. All our efforts, here. How can we give it up?"

"We have no choice." It was Dr. Lin. "What's more important, the safety of all of us or a few plowed fields and unfinished buildings?"

"It's more than that," Captain Hudson said. "We've all sunk our life savings into getting here. Where would we go? They don't want us on Prantax Beta, and even if they did—it's always been an unlucky colony. That plague . . ."

"The plague is history now." Cleo's voice had an edge of impatience. "They've recovered, and Ceti is no longer a menace, though the Betans will never admit it. I think they'll take us in. They'd have to—they're responsible for us being on this ghost-ridden rock."

"Yes, and they didn't warn us." Tim's voice again. "We could report them to SEF. The Federation Court would have plenty to say."

Arnie sounded unconvinced. "If we could prove that they knew about the danger here. Maybe they didn't."

"Hah!" Cleo retorted. "They knew, all right. They started a colony here themselves once. Now we know why it failed." She lowered her voice,

conspiratorial. "The Betans wanted an established base on Primus; wanted it so badly they
duped us into putting our lives on the line for
them. An offense that could get them inter-
dicted. We could threaten to expose them. Pressure them to accept us on Beta. Or even to let us
take the *Santa Maria* out again."

"Fat chance." This time Captain Hudson
snorted. "Not with those hyperdrives. They cost
a fortune, and what guarantee would they have
they'd get the ship back?"

"They could send their own crew." Arnie appeared to have switched sides. "But we'd need
clearance from SEF."

"There's nothing in this quadrant . . ."

"Beta might not be as bad as we've heard. . ."

"What about the other pole, here? Shouldn't
we investigate . . ."

The discussion continued, but the whispers
began to buzz and Morgan stopped listening.
She didn't know what they decided. Time passed:
suffocating time. Arnie pulled back the curtain,
and the others were gone.

Dr. Lin's head appeared in the doorway. "Good,
Morgan, you're awake." She came back inside.
"Let's go for a walk." She turned to Arnie. "She
needs the exercise, and God, this tent's a sauna.
I'll look after her."

Arnie nodded, and Morgan heaved herself to
her feet. She walked slowly with Cleo through
the compound, captive and warder. Her straw
sandals were as heavy on her feet as nailed
boots. Her body to her was gross: her belly monstrous, her legs swollen with thick ropy veins,
the smell of her sweat rank and nauseating.

The fiery eye of Prantax glowed between the
distant peaks, and she turned her face to its
purifying heat. If it could burn her, she thought,
melt away her substance until she was as incor-

poreal as the whisper people, then she could be free from her imprisoning flesh.

"Snap out of it, Morgan," Cleo said, shaking her. "Did you feel one of those phantoms? We'd better go back inside."

"No, not in there. I can't breathe in that tent. I need air."

She dragged the protesting doctor to the compound's edge where the ring of guards patrolled. Only two figures were in sight. Dr. Lin stopped protesting, and with a look of wonder started across the field toward the mountains.

Dain Temko was the closest guard. He tackled the frail doctor before she had gone a hundred yards, but she struggled with such force that he called to his partner for help. While they were both occupied the whisperer came to Morgan and she walked unobserved out of camp.

She moved with surprising ease over the rough stubble of the abandoned field, then like a deer through the wiry grass up to the first slopes of the mountain.

The whisperer avoided the trail, leading her instead across a treacherous incline of loose rock where she scrambled on all fours, into a ravine where she was well hidden. She moved in a trance, unaware of her physical condition, of the sharp stones that filled her sandals, of her bruised knees and scratched hands. She seemed to walk on a cushion of air, conscious only of the tantalizing whisper that promised escape and wonderful freedom for her and her child.

Sweat poured down her face as she pulled herself by handholds up steep grades that even Arnie would never have dared. She knew no fear, except of being caught before she could be transformed into something ethereal, clean, and pure.

She had no sense of time or distance, but she knew she was near her goal when she came out

of the ravine onto a broad plateau. It embraced
the stone of the mountain on one side and fell to
nothing on the other, a step where one could
walk off into the sky. The air was thin and she
felt marvelously light and free, but her body
was still a husk that hampered her. A cocoon
that she had outgrown but to which she was
still attached.

She stretched out her arms and tried to shake
off the confining weight, but it clung, anchoring
her to the ground when without it she knew she
could fly. The whisperers swooped in pairs and
flocks above her head, and she strained toward
them, lighter and lighter, until she knew that
with a final thrust she could be over the edge of
the plateau and floating free.

She could be transparent as air and light as a
Midian puffbird. Her child would float beside
her and they would know and love one another.
She seemed to see her discarded husk far below
on the rocks, but it was nothing to her, a cast-off
garment.

She reveled in the sensation of flight, in the
wordless affinity with her child, in the clarity of
her vision which discerned the colors of the air,
the texture of the clouds, and the strata of the
rocks. She dipped tentatively into communion
with the other whisperers and marveled at the
riches that awaited her there.

The valley glistened like a jewel far below,
pure as the mountains except for the excres-
cence of the human settlement. She pitied the
fleshly creatures that moved there so clumsily:
struggling, earthbound, contaminating the air
with their emanations, the soil with their feeble
scratchings. The compound was a rubbish heap,
fouling the clean green carpet of the valley, and
the building site was an abomination, a dull red
wound upon the living earth.

When she swooped closer she was repulsed by

the messy force of their emotions. One, though—the bulky figure running frantically across the fields—stirred something in her.

She remembered. She had made a promise, and it bound her to the earth, to her body, to the fetters of humanity.

She lowered her arms and moved away from the cliff's edge. She was very tired, and sank down upon the hot stones to wait for rescue. She knew that she should be breathing thanks, but a vision haunted her, and the tears that filled her eyes were as much for her loss as for her preservation.

"We're leaving Primus," Arnie said. "It's been decided." Morgan had been delirious for several days, but now her head was clear. She started to sit up.

Cleo stopped her. "Do you feel well enough to talk?"

"Doc says it's a miracle you didn't miscarry," Arnie said. He smoothed back her matted hair. "From now on . . ."

"Don't worry," Morgan said. "I'm not leaving this bed. You'll have to carry me onto the shuttle. But where are we going? To Beta?" Her initial joy evaporated. Beta's history was well known: an unhappy colony plagued by drought and disease and periodic revolts against an oppressive government.

Arnie read her dismay. "It's one option. The other is Epsilon Eridani. The third planet. It's a premium colony, but since this is an emergency they'll let a limited number of us in on hardship status."

"The Betans will let us have the *Santa Maria*? I can't believe it. What prompted this generosity?"

Arnie grinned. "Blackmail. Hudson sent a dozen helexes, and they caved in." He held up his hand. "I'll explain it all later. But before you get too excited—they're keeping the hyper-drive units. They'll give us an operable fusion drive and install it. It's the best deal we could get."

Again Morgan's hopes were dashed. "Fusion! It'll take years to get to Eridani III through normal space."

"Six years, our time."

Morgan groaned. With hyperdrive, they could have made it in weeks. Still . . . "It's a beautiful planet," she said. "Or so I've heard. Do you know what they named it?"

"New Terra. Not very original, but you'll have to admit it has a promising ring."

"It does—but six years!"

Arnie looked sober. "It's that or Prantax Beta. Think about it carefully, because I want you to choose. I'm the one who brought us here, and look what I got us into. This time the decision is going to be yours."

She grimaced. "Thanks a heap." She turned to Cleo, who was preparing to leave. "What have you decided?"

"I'm going to Beta. Most of us are, so there won't be more than a hundred on the *Santa*. It should be fairly comfortable."

"But who'll deliver me, then?"

"Krista. She's a competent midwife—I trained her myself, on Earth."

"You've decided already?" Arnie gaped in astonishment.

"No," Morgan said. "I just want to be clear on both alternatives." What a choice, she thought. Six years of confinement to get to an Eden, or a lifetime on another marginal world.

She would take however much time she had to make a final decision. In her heart, however, she already knew.

*   *   *

Morgan poured more coffee. "I'm beginning to run down, Mr. Billingsgate. Haven't you found out enough?"

He accepted a cup. "Morgan—may I call you that? Why do you resent this interview?"

"I don't." She checked herself. "Well . . . maybe I do, just a little. I'd like to know what it is you're looking for. A 'psychological profile,' you say? Well, I've had batteries of tests, and passed them all. Sure, I had a breakdown on Primus, but I recovered. I'm no nut case."

Billingsgate held up a hand. "I know that. Your latest evaluation—the one from New Terra—is extremely favorable. But Valdisport, I gather, is an insular community."

"And you think the psychologist wasn't impartial?"

"Such judgments are always somewhat subjective. I prefer to make my own."

Morgan damped her reaction; the man held her future in balance. "Those were difficult times," she said evenly. "For all of us."

"Your family, you mean?"

"Yes."

"Tell me about the boy. I understand there was a problem."

She nodded, remembering. Twenty years of teaching hadn't prepared her for one small bundle of neuroses. Not when she felt responsible. . . .

VII. New Terra

Matt hung back in the doorway of the bubble-hut as his brother Dan and Eric McLean raced off into the field of blooming skrill. He was a solemn-looking waif of a boy, undersized for his six years, his thin face pinched with the effort of marshaling the courage to follow them.

The meadow stretched as far before him as he could see, a vast golden carpet broken only by the squat huts, the skeletal framework of the new houses, and the brown plowed patches that tiny figures were steadily laboring to enlarge. To the west glinted a line of blue darker than the sky, and behind the hut, where Matt studiously refused to look, spread the pod forests.

"Come on, come on!" Danny shouted, beckoning as he ran. "We're all going to the lake. Last one there's a digger in a hole."

Matt drew back farther into the hut, his resolution shattered by the image that formed in his mind of that shining expanse of water, more exposed even than the meadow, more open to the strange light sky, to the blazing eye of the sun, to the outside.

The boy was ashamed of his fear. All the other children, Earth-born, delighted in the outside. He, however, had known no world but that of the *Santa Maria*. No one else, he knew, could possibly understand how he felt, and he hadn't tried to explain it. Only his mother suspected, and he had promised her that he would go out today with the others, but when he looked again through the doorway all the nightmare terrors of open space darkened the sunny meadow. Not even the thought of Morgan's disappointment could force him out *there*.

Matt shivered and closed the door firmly. The walls curved over and around him, and he breathed more easily. He pulled down the window shades and he could almost imagine that he was back on the colony starship, in the snug family cabin where they had lived safely enclosed as people should.

His mother had never been too busy for him then—for lessons and stories and hours of cozy talk. He had even joined in sometimes with Danny and Dee and the other older kids in their wild corridor games. Everyone had been so close then, all the families together, not spread out as they were on this endless flat plain, out of sight and out of hearing and much too far apart to touch.

Maybe they would go back, Matt daydreamed, taking comfort from his father's reassurances that the *Santa Maria* waited in orbit in case the promises of Eridani III should prove deceptive. Maybe they would all live again secure within thick metal walls.

The bubble-hut had walls of thin plasteen. Matt could sense the open space pressing on him through them. He crawled under his bunk and pulled the blanket down over the side to shut him in completely. His thumb found his mouth and he curled himself into a tight ball.

The stamping of feet and his father's gruff voice awakened him. He removed the thumb but continued to lie very still.

"That was a good morning's work. Thanks for

helping—we'll make a field hand out of you yet."

His mother answered with a light laugh. "That'll be the day! But God, Arnie, that skrill reseeds itself almost as fast as we pull it out. Do you think our crops will do as well?"

"The ag teams say they will. I'm going to start planting tomorrow." A spoon clinked against a cup, and Arnie sipped noisily. "This afternoon I'll try to finish the roof on the house. We'll want to be in it before the rains come."

Matt heard the sound of pans rattling, packets snipped open, pouring, stirring. "I can't wait for fresh vegetables," Morgan said.

Chairs scraped on the floor. Matt could imagine them sitting at the pullout table.

Morgan broke the silence. "Did anyone think about lunch for the kids? Maybe I'd better take some of this over."

"Kai's in charge," Arnie said. "And Krista. We don't have to worry."

"They must be having a glorious time." Morgan's voice sounded wistful. "And it's so good for them, after all those years cooped up. But do you think—maybe I'd better go check on Matt. See how he's doing."

"Hey—go ahead," Arnie said, laughing. "I know you just want an excuse to get in that water yourself. Matt's okay. Kai is a trained lifeguard, and they've all got to learn to swim."

"I know." She breathed a loud sigh. "Matt's got to get over being so timid. But I never expected he'd react the way he has to leaving the ship. I was so relieved this morning when he said he'd go with the other kids."

"I told you, he'll be okay." Arnie's voice had an edge. "The boy just needed a little time to adjust. High time he came out of it, too. We've enough to cope with without that kind of problem."

Scraping of chairs again, the sloshing of dishes in the pan. Morgan spoke: "I'll take the flitter, then, and go look in on them at the lake. Then I'll come help you on the house."

"Good." The door opened, and Arnie whistled. "Look at that sky, will you? It's hard to think the weather will ever change. But according to the Valdisport people . . ."

The door closed, and their voices faded. Matt curled himself tighter, his heart beating wildly. His mother would find that he wasn't at the lake, hadn't gone. *We've enough to cope with without that kind of problem.* He could imagine his father's burst of hurt, quick anger when he discovered the problem still there.

"Maybe you'd be sorry if I were gone," he whispered to himself. "Both of you." He had never been able to please his father, but lately, ever since the landing, his mother had been looking at him in that puzzled way, too. As if he were some kind of a freak, just because he wanted to stay inside. She was always working now. Digging up skrill or drying the sour waterweeds that she insisted were good to eat or helping Dad with the new house.

The bubble-hut was bad enough to live in, surrounded by all the open, with those horrible trees creeping up behind it, but at least it was small and when they were all together at night with the lamp burning and nothing to see outside it was almost like the *Santa Maria.* But the house . . . it had separate rooms for everyone and enormous windows that let in the sky. "Light! Space!" Mother had exclaimed the last time he had been there with her, when she had danced around the corner beams and the rough board walls. "Matt, isn't it wonderful, and don't we deserve it, after what we've been through?"

He couldn't tell her then how much he hated it. He had never been able to. They didn't talk much anymore, and he couldn't tell her anything. Dan was "such a help, working almost like a man," Dad said often, and Delila, at the school in Port Blue, was "a credit to the family." But not Matt, the baby. He had made excuse after excuse to stay inside the hut until he knew that even his mother no longer believed in his sore throats or stomachaches.

"Just plain laziness," his father had called it at first, as if his shaming could work an effect. But finally he had stopped and left Matt alone. Mother had, too, until yesterday when she had come in by herself, slipped off from her work just to talk to him, and he had made the promise.

And now he had broken it. He crawled out of his burrow. He couldn't let them find him here, hiding like a sneaky coward. If only he could disappear. He had to get away, even if it meant out there, in the open.

He cracked the door, and fear choked him. He *had* to, before they returned. There was no place to hide in the meadow, and the kids were at the lake. Blindly he turned and stumbled toward the ragged line of purple trees.

I mustn't panic, Morgan told herself. Matt could be anywhere; there's no reason to think disaster.

Nevertheless, she overshot her descent angle and landed the flitter much too far from the house, with an unskillful jolt that brought a yelp of dismay from Danny.

As they sprinted across the skrill, Morgan waved Arnie down from the roof. He waited for them in the patch of shade provided by the projecting balcony, frowning and twisting his hands as if he already knew.

"He wasn't there," Morgan blurted. "He hadn't gone with the others at all." Her hair, cut short for coolness, stood up in a windblown disarray, and even with her sunburn her face had the look of pallor. "But where could he be?" She forgot her resolve to be calm, glaring at her stepson. "Why didn't you come tell us right away that Matt wasn't with you?"

Danny shifted his gawky fifteen-year-old frame. He studied his toes in the open sandals. "I thought he was following us." He looked up, with a flash of belligerence. "And anyway, he's always stayed by himself in the hut before. Scared to go out. Why would I think it'd be any different today?"

"He's right." Arnie silenced Morgan's protest. "It's not Danny's fault; don't jump on him. And don't get all upset yet. We don't know that anything's happened to Matt. Maybe we ought to be relieved that he's finally gotten over his phobia."

Morgan choked off a sharp retort. Arnie had never understood her special concern for Matt. It wasn't that she loved him more than the twins, but they were almost adults now—assured and independent—while Matt had never gotten over needing her. But Arnie was right—she shouldn't take out her tensions on Danny. With an effort, she regained control. "You will help me search, won't you? I'll talk to everyone here on the meadow, see if anyone's seen him. If you could look around in the woods . . ."

"Matt wouldn't go there; he hates the pod forest," Danny said.

Arnie's mouth tightened. "He hates everything out here." He glanced at Morgan, and tempered his tone. "But apparently he's had a change of heart. About time, too. Sure, I'll go. Danny, you can come with me."

Morgan watched them walk to the flitter. Danny would soon be as tall as his father, but he was boyishly slim while Arnie was broad-shouldered and muscular. They had the same straight-backed stride, sure and competent. It seemed to Morgan that Arnie could do anything he set his mind to, and Danny was of the same mold. She stifled a gasp as Arnie let the boy take the controls, and closed her eyes. When she looked again the flitter was making a wobbly ascent.

Morgan made a circuit of the huts and half-built houses, questioning everyone. When she had no luck she went farther, to the sawmill at the edge of the woods and to the sprawling sheds of the shuttle camp. The golden pollen rose in a cloud around her ankles as she tramped the skrill, and the sun caressed her shoulders with a gentle warmth. If only Matt could have shared her pleasure in this new homeworld, she thought. They had shared so much during the long claustrophobic years, had been so close. But he'll come around, she told herself. He'll be all right. She clung to Arnie's conjecture: a change of heart. After all, it had happened to others.

But no one had seen Matt, and Morgan's assurance began to crumble. She was waiting in the hut when Arnie and Danny returned from an equally fruitless search. Arnie's gray-bearded face was sternly set. "That little nitwit. He knew the rules. *We don't leave the compound area alone.* When I get hold of him . . ."

Arnie's anger, Morgan knew, was a mask for his fear. Her own clutched coldly at her heart.

The refugees had been allotted an unsettled plain on the temperate plateau of South Valdis-land. Though exploring parties had surveyed the bordering wooded areas and up into the mountains, after Primus Morgan was well aware of possible undiscovered dangers. She thought of pits and sinkholes and carnivorous animals, of poisonous plants and insects that could have eluded the survey; and as the shadows lengthened she thought of cold and darkness and the terrors of night.

"I'll get help," Arnie said. "Organize a full-scale search. We'll find him before dark."

Crews went through every structure on the meadow, over the logged area of the forest, and as far into the interior as Matt could conceivably have gotten on foot—and turned up nothing. "But you know that forest," Arnie said. "How thick the undergrowth is in parts. If a person wanted to hide in there . . ."

"Or if he were hurt," Morgan said. She busied herself making coffee for the search parties as they straggled in.

Krista Ramsey, accepting a cup, looked at her sharply. She said nothing, but Morgan knew what the doctor was thinking. "Morgan, the child needs help," Krista had said as far back as Matt's third year, when he had shrunk from the viewports on the *Santa Maria* and screamed in his sleep after astronomy lessons.

Krista served now as their medical resource person, but her formal training had been in psychiatry. She had a smooth, mahogany-hued complexion and keen eyes that projected the kind of awareness that always made Morgan feel uncomfortably exposed. Matt hadn't taken to her, either. After a couple of sessions he had cried so much in protest that Morgan had called off the analysis. So what if he feared the stars? she thought. She hadn't been so wild about committing herself to the years in space, either.

If there had been any other choice worth considering, she wouldn't have done it. The colonists who had chosen the long journey were by far the more youthful of the original group. Except for Arnie, everyone else on the *Santa Maria* was at least twenty years younger than Morgan. All the friends of their own age—Hudson and

Grant and Cleo and Lupe—had elected to go to Beta.

The young people had organized the life on the starship according to their energies, and Morgan had been glad for the excuse of her pregnancy to escape from most of the frenetic activity. Primus had left her depleted physically and emotionally. She knew that she had been more than a little mad, at the end, and she needed seclusion and quiet to heal—features in short supply on the *Santa*. She hadn't minded when Beth McLean had set up the school and staffed it with her own friends, or when the twins spent less and less time in the family cabin. Or even when Arnie had begun to fill his hours with all kinds of taped courses and interminable planning sessions with the newly elected leaders. Morgan had searched the library herself for every disk and bookspool on infant care. Absorbed in her private world, she had been able to maintain a bubble of isolation.

Matt had been a high-strung child from birth, and later he was given to unexplained anxieties that only she could soothe. Fortunately, she had had all the time in the world for him. "Morgan, you're an angel of patience," Beth had said admiringly. "To give up so much . . ."

But she hadn't given up anything except tiresome ship duties, Krista's boring groups, and uninspired lectures on farming and mining and water systems. Rocks and sewage! Matt had been perfectly content as long as she was with him, and while he played she had whiled away dreamy hours reading or listening to music or painting her miniatures.

Only Krista Ramsey had looked at her in that peculiar way.

And sometimes Arnie. She knew that he wished she could be more like the other women—like Beth, plain though she was, who organized nurseries and schools and actually wanted to learn about rocks. There had even been a time, after Tim McLean's death, when she had wondered if Arnie's admiration for the pioneer paragon had become something more dangerous. But Beth had married the engineer Santos, and Arnie had come back to her.

Krista coughed, and Morgan was conscious of her continued scrutiny. "Matt hadn't gotten any better, then?" the psychiatrist finally said.

Morgan felt the heat in her face. "No, for the last week he wouldn't go out of the hut. That's why I can't understand . . . "

"Morgan!" Beth Santos, rushing in , embraced her. "I was out with the mineral team and I just heard. How can I help?"

Beth's bulging pregnancy strained the material of her coverall. She had been the first to conceive, after the sterility of the space flight, already showing by the time they had finished their indoctrination at Port Blue. Morgan eyed her with alarm and pulled out a chair. "We've plenty of people out searching," she said. "There's really nothing for you to do now."

Beth continued standing.

"Sit down. Please," Morgan urged. "And if you've been prospecting all day, hadn't you better get home and rest?"

Beth grinned. "Don't let me make you nervous; I've never felt better." She tossed her head, and her thick braid of hair swung from one shoulder to the other. "At least let Danny sleep over for the night. Get him out of this." The din in the hut had increased to pandemonium as more and more figures crowded in. "And don't worry about Matt. Probably just a kid's prank. Remember when the twins and Eric 'ran away' on the *Santa*, and we turned the ship upside down? And they'd gotten up to the bridge and were scared to come out?"

"Sure, and thanks for the offer. I'll tell Danny."
Morgan tried to echo Beth's confidence, but it
was a poor veil for her growing dread. Behind
her a group of men talked of dragging the lake.
When she turned, they fell silent. She ran outside and leaned against a wall strut, her heart
pounding.

Krista followed her and pressed a capsule into
her hand. "Take it." she insisted. "It'll relax you,
help you get through this."

Tranquilized, Morgan watched more searchers
come and go. The moons rose, and she joined a
group in the airsled that flooded the forest with
searchlights and projected her amplified voice,
calling.

They returned her to the hut, which was mercifully empty. The sedative wore off, and Morgan paced. The night grew darker as the first
moon sank below the horizon. She heard Arnie's
voice and ran to the door.

"Thanks. We'll start again at daybreak. Sure.
I understand. Any time you can spare." Arnie
detached himself from the knot of figures and
entered the hut. "We can't do any more tonight,
stumbling around out there blind." He slumped
into a chair. "It's not cold. If he's found a place
to hole up, he'll be all right until morning."

"How can you ..." Morgan seized Arnie's
beamer. "I'll go out myself and search!"

"Hey—hold on there." He caught her arm in a
painful grip. "You think I'm unfeeling? Hell,
Morgan, I'm as worried as you are, but we've
done all we can for now. You go out there half-
baked like that and we'll end up searching
for you too."

She looked away. He was right, of course.
"It's just that—I wouldn't be able to sleep
anyway."

His face changed, softened. "I can take care of
that." With a hand on each shoulder Arnie guided

her to her cot. She sat stiffly while his fingers massaged her back. "Feel good?" His beard tickled her cheek.

He can't be, she thought. Not at a time like this.

"Relax," he said. "It's not often we get a chance to be alone."

At first she felt too defeated to protest, but when her body reacted in shocked rejection she twisted out of his reach. She felt nothing but hatred for him: a brute, a stranger.

Arnie sat slumped, his face to the wall. The silence between them stretched unbearably, until Arnie choked on a strangled hiccup. His shoulders began to heave, and Morgan felt her own tightness melt.

"I thought . . . we could help each other," he whispered.

She touched the taut cords of his neck. Perhaps they could. . . .

Morgan disengaged herself from Arnie's sleeping weight at the first gray light. She had lain tense through the early hours, tortured by phantoms: Matt on the *Santa Maria*, following her everywhere, loving and comforting and filling her needs too well; Krista, accusing; Matt's frightened eyes, after they landed, and herself so relieved, so happy, and with so impossibly much to do.

They had erupted upon the planet like reprieved prisoners. To Morgan, who had almost forgotten how it was to live freely under open skies, the hospitable world was a wonder. How easy it had been to minimize the one distressing surprise.

She should have anticipated it, she told herself now. Krista had done so, she was sure of it, the way she had looked at her and Matt with that clinical gaze that saw into a person's soul.

"I couldn't help it," Morgan protested into her pillow. Matt had been such a miracle—a beautiful and healthy baby, after all she had been through on Primus—that she could never have left him, crying, in the nursery. And how could she force him to sit miserably in Beth's school when she could so easily teach him herself? Krista had said nothing when Morgan hadn't followed her suggestions, but Morgan had avoided her nonetheless. Someday the doctor would expose her, Morgan knew. For her deceits and her acts of selfishness that no one else perceived. She shuddered and pulled the pillow over her head.

Morgan's guilt cried for relief, for action, and she rose and dressed quickly. The room smelled of sweat and stale sex, and she pushed open the window as far as it would go. Arnie awoke, and took one look at her strained face. "God, Morgan, didn't you get any sleep at all?"

She stared at him, unable to speak.

He offered awkward comfort. "It's all right, hon. We'll find him. You've got to be brave."

Morgan pulled herself together. Arnie thought her concern was all for Matt, and she wouldn't want him to know otherwise. She splashed her face with cold water and occupied herself with morning chores. Breakfast. Busy hands and no dangerous thoughts.

Her supply of grains was getting low, she noticed, weighing with her hands the bag of barley. "I wonder how long these rations will last." She stirred the gruel and ladled it into two bowls.

Arnie patted her arm. "We're in fair shape. We've enough to see us through until we get our own crop."

"And if we don't?"

"Then we'll have a decision—the emergency stores on the *Santa*, or apply to Valdisport for relief. But it won't come to that. We'll make it, if our luck holds out."

"Luck?" Morgan started. How could he say that?

Arnie looked as though he would like to recall his words, but he said nothing.

They sat down at the table, both silent. A frown creased Arnie's forehead. He hesitated a moment longer, then plunged ahead. "You *are* happy here, aren't you, Morgan? I mean, aside from this trouble about Matt? For so long, on the *Santa*, I was afraid we'd made another terrible mistake."

"Because of me?" The fear surfaced again. *He knows*, she thought.

Arnie's words came slowly. "You were so . . . different. So withdrawn. It wasn't much of a choice I offered you, was it? I know how hard it was for you in the first place, giving up the life you'd planned on Earth. And then that frightening business on Primus. Believe me, I've thought a hundred times that I shouldn't have let you do it." He examined his fingernails. "I'd hoped that, since we landed here . . . You've seemed more content, and you've worked so hard, but still I've wondered . . ."

She turned away, to hide her relief. Let him wonder, she thought. It wouldn't hurt him to remember his responsibility, to feel a little guilt, himself. Back on the *Santa* it had been all that had kept him from Beth, she was sure.

Arnie waited for her response, more vulnerable than he had been in years, and Morgan was suddenly tired of manipulative games. She could easily give Arnie the reassurance he sought, but she had never entirely gotten over the Beth episode. She hesitated, and the moment was lost. "If only Matt is all right . . ." she temporized, not quite answering him.

Arnie's face closed. He returned to their immediate concern. "We'll start searching the woods again right away; it's the only place he can possibly be."

By the time they finished eating, a crowd was gathered outside. Arnie divided them into teams, fanning out in a pattern designed to cover as much of the wilderness as thoroughly as possible. Morgan went with Danny and Eric, moving in a sweeping line as they entered the shadows of the forest.

Beyond the logged-off area the pod trees grew thickly, their gnarled blue-gray trunks planted in the earth like monstrous legs. Dark purple umbrellas of fleshy leaves and hanging seedpods blocked out the light overhead; and underfoot, exposed roots that had pushed their way to the surface made walking treacherous.

Morgan felt an unreasoning aversion to the trees. The forest was the only feature of their immediate environment that affected her so. The skrill meadow, the lake, even the distant mountains were not too un-Earthlike, but the enveloping pod forest was as alien as any dark world she had visited.

Strangely enough, she thought, Matt had seemed more comfortable there than anywhere else on the plateau, before she had infected him with her own fears. She remembered the first time they had gone there together. Matt had clung tightly to her hand when they crossed the meadow, but under the trees she had had to call him back to her. The branches had then been alive with flittering web-winged flyers and the underbrush with the foxlike, furry burrowers they called diggers.

To her it had been a lair of phantoms. They had stayed well in shouting distance of the logging crews, but still Morgan had been overcome by panic. Matt had come to her quickly, and she had held him until the thudding of her heart subsided. They hadn't stayed long in the forest, and when they left she could tell that Matt was seeing it as she did.

He wouldn't go near it again, and after a few days he wouldn't go outside at all.

As Morgan reflected back, the lowering trees seemed to accuse her. Matt had been her lifeline, and how had she repaid him? Everything, it seemed, that she had done for him was wrong. She tried to make herself into an automaton as she searched, to avoid thinking, but all the time Matt's frightened eyes were with her. If she could only have another chance. . . .

There were no signs of life in the forest, the creatures apparently driven to their nests and dens by the noise of the searchers. Morgan proceeded with methodical care. Beneath the thick-laced branches of the larger trees there was little undergrowth, but around the newer trees and in small sun-dappled patches where the overhead foliage was thin, viny bushes grew in waist-high clumps. Morgan tore them apart, one by one, dreading each time what she might find. She called intermittently, adding her voice to that of the boys, hearing far off the faint shouts of the others.

When Arnie's whistle recalled them, Morgan was amazed to find it was midday. She blinked at the sun and slumped down upon a log at the forested edge of the clearing. Retreating figures swam dizzily before her.

Arnie came, and her vision cleared. "Do we have to stop?" she protested, dismayed that everyone was leaving. "They could have brought lunches." She pulled a crumbled food bar from her pocket.

"They'll be back," he said. "Some of them."

"Some?" She straightened abruptly. "What do you mean? We're not giving up?"

"Of course not. But you know, we can't stop

all our other projects. If those fields aren't planted before the rains ... I don't have to tell you. We've already lost a morning."

"Not to mention a son."

He tightened his lips. "Morgan, Danny and I are going to put in an hour's work in the field, then we'll be back here. You can't do anything by yourself—why don't you go home for a while. You look exhausted."

"No, I'll wait here," she insisted. "As soon as someone shows up, I'll go back into the woods."

He glanced there, briefly, and Morgan saw the pain of a man torn. "Yes, of course," he said. "But don't go alone."

She nodded. "And Arnie. About this morning— what you asked me. No, I don't regret coming here. I'm sorry about a lot of other things, but not that."

His kiss would have repaid her, if she had not been doing penance. She watched without feeling his straight back retreating into the field, his feet lost in the drift of pollen. Then she turned and stared into the forest, where swollen branches dangled bursting purple pods. "I've done that much," she whispered. "What else now?"

A shadow fell over her. Krista Ramsey had approached silently and sat beside her. A lump formed inside Morgan's chest. Now it's coming, she thought. The condemnation. She would not look at Krista.

The doctor, however, seemed unaware of Morgan's state. "It's a fecund world," she said in a conversational manner. "The skrill, the trees, the diggers—always bearing. Us, too. Besides Beth, I know of half a dozen pregnancies since the landing."

"Precipitate, aren't they?" Morgan said. Not long ago her own empty womb had reproached her, but now she was glad.

"No, it's our instinct for survival," Krista said.

"Perhaps we'd be better off without it. Perhaps this planet isn't so hospitable after all." Morgan's voice reflected her bitterness.

Krista placed her hand on Morgan's. "You know it isn't the planet," she said.

"Oh, so it's me. The destroyer. I was waiting for you to say that." She still refused to look at Krista, hoarding her last scrap of inviolate dignity.

"I wasn't going to say that at all," the younger woman said. "You have a stronger instinct for survival than anyone else here. And I think you may have given some of that to Matt. I wouldn't despair about him."

"What do you mean?" Morgan finally met Krista's gaze. To her surprise she found no judgment there. Only compassion and—she could scarcely believe it—understanding.

"You and Matt. That incredible bond should work for you, now." It was a statement, with no tinge of criticism. "Let's go into the forest again, just the two of us. Now that the others have left, with their tramping and shouting, we may have a chance to find a frightened little boy."

The lump in Morgan's chest began to melt. Krista pulled her to her feet. "Let's go, while we're still alone."

"But . . . how? Where do we start?"

"Shhh! Follow me, and keep still."

The two women walked quietly under the canopy, disturbing the vines and leaves as little as possible. When they were well out of sight of the clearing, Krista stopped. "Just listen," she whispered. "Sit down—over there—and see if you can pick up someting."

Krista leaned against a tree and Morgan sat on a rotted windfall stump. The forest showed indications of returning life—a pod falling heavily to the ground, a web-wing fluttering through

the branches. Morgan strained her senses, but
she heard no human sound.

Krista signaled, and they moved deeper into
the cover. Morgan sat again, waiting. A few diggers ventured from their hiding places, saw the
strangers, and disappeared. Morgan called to
Matt, silently, willing him to answer.

After an hour of moving from spot to spot,
fruitlessly, Morgan began to chafe. She stared at
a clump of undergrowth that appeared undis-
turbed from earlier searches and could barely
restrain herself from breaking into it.

Krista anticipated her. "No, that's what we
did before," she whispered. "And it was the
wrong approach. Be patient a little longer."

A sleek-furred digger glided from between two
thick trunks and then vanished as completely as
if it had been swallowed by the mossy humus.

"Imagine Matt in here, alone and afraid,"
Krista whispered.

It wasn't hard. The panic hovered, and she
was Matt, searching for comfort.

The diggers. Yes, he'd try to get close to one,
try to follow it, Morgan thought. Was it possible
. . . "How large are the digger burrows?" She
couldn't keep her voice steady.

Krista placed a finger to her lips, but her eyes
were alive with excitement. She described with
her hands a meter-wide oval. "Large enough,"
she whispered. "And the entrances are completely
hidden, unless you know where to look."

A whiskery brown face peered from behind an
exposed root. Krista and Morgan arose and approached as quietly as they could. The face disappeared, and they felt over every inch of the
earth between the trees, then went over it again,
digging with their fingers. They found no con-
cealed tunnel, but Morgan was not discouraged.

They moved on, watching and waiting. Though
the diggers remained elusive, Morgan remem-

bered how numerous she had once seen them in that very area. Somewhere near, she knew, there must be a warren of underground dens.

Matt heard the scrabbling and shifted position, moving his head away from the opening. The tiny digger that was curled against his chest moved too, snuggling a sticky nose underneath his chin.

A shower of sticks and dirt fell on him. The baby digger scurried into an interior tunnel, and Matt squeezed himself as small as possible. The last time it had been a large angry father, hissing and bristling. Matt had tried to get out then, but climbing up had proved more difficult than sliding down into the hole. Every time he had managed to wriggle into the entry tunnel he had started another dirt slide, until now the opening was almost blocked.

The digger house had been such a cozy safe nest, except for the smell, until he had gotten hungry and thirsty. Now his whole body ached from his cramped position, his pants were soaked with pee, and there was no way to get out. He'd been here forever, it seemed, and sometimes, when he woke from dreams that he was back on the *Santa*, he couldn't even remember what it was like outside.

Once he had thought he heard muffled shouts and had tried to answer, but all he had done was frighten his pet. Now the shouts came again, and he scarcely dared breathe.

"Matt! Matt! Are you there?" This time it was his mother's voice, no mistake, and she was at the top of the hole. At first he didn't move— couldn't—didn't even want to try. But then she called again, and it seemed to him that he was curled up in his very first bed, the web-cradle one, and it was morning and time for him to get up. Then, somehow. it was even before that. . . .

He twisted around until he could get his head and shoulders into the tunnel, and stretched up one arm. "It's me," he shouted. "Here I am!"

Morgan squeezed the fingers, to reassure him. The tunnel, though, looked choked and impossibly narrow. "The other hand, Matt," she called down, and when it appeared, she and Krista pulled.

The hands moved only a few inches. "He's stuck," Krista said. "You hold on to him while I enlarge the hole."

Morgan squatted and braced her heels against an upthrust root. While Krista carefully removed soil she grasped Matt by the wrists and struggled to keep him from slipping back.

Krista worked until both her arms were buried in the hole. "Here's his head," she gasped. "I'll protect his face. Pull, now, as hard as you can!"

Morgan braced herself again and strained.

Matt whimpered, resisting her, pulling against her.

She could feel his pain and his terror. Her breath came in ragged gasps as she fought him, until his agony exploded within her and she fell back, writhing.

Someone howled; from far away, it seemed.

"It's all right, Morgan, we're almost there." Krista was wiping Matt's face. His head was out of the hole, and part of his shoulders. "Just one more pull, and he'll be free." She reached down and rotated the shoulders while Morgan repositioned herself for another effort.

He was out, caked with dirt and crying in piercing wails. Morgan felt him all over to be sure he was unharmed, then cradled him and rocked him and mingled her own tears with his. She was aware of nothing but her overpowering relief and her love for the squalling newborn infant.

Finally reality returned: the forest, Krista, her six-year-old son curled up awkwardly on her lap. "Will he be all right?" she asked.

Krista smiled. "I'm sure of it." She gently examined Matt. "If he's too heavy, I'll help you carry him back."

"No, I can manage." Morgan kept her arms tightly around Matt while Krista helped her up.

"I'll talk to Arnie," Krista said as they walked. "Let Matt stay in bed until he wants to get up and out. I don't think it'll be long, this time."

"This time? You mean—'

"That we did it all wrong, before. When we landed here and expected Matt to react like the rest of us. But then, he was our first experience with a ship-born."

"So it wasn't just me!" Morgan felt relieved of such an enormous weight that Matt was feather-light in her arms. She would have hugged Krista, if she had been able.

They came out of the woods into the sunlight. A haze hung over the skrill, shimmering into golden waves on the far horizon. *New Terra*, Morgan thought with an ache of happiness.

Tiny figures appeared, coming toward them. She recognized Arnie and Danny and began to run, Matt still cradled in her arms.

Epilogue

"Is Matt all right now?" Billingsgate asked.

Morgan nodded. "Perfectly. He and Arnie are here on the station, too—thanks to a bumper crop of soygrain. We just saw Dee and Danny off Earthside, to the Academy, so the three of us are free to travel."

Billingsgate rubbed his chin. "Matt is . . . ten now, right? Wouldn't it be traumatic for him to be uprooted again?"

"Dr. Ramsey doesn't think so. And Matt's wild to go."

"What about Arnie?"

"He wants to come with me, wherever I'm posted, and look for security work. He was getting as restless on New Terra as I was. We decided that neither of is quite ready for retirement."

"You'd give up your homestead?"

"Oh, no! We love every acre. We'll go back, when we *are* ready." She took a deep breath. "So what's your answer? Can you tell me now, or do I have to wait?"

He smiled. "You've dispelled all my reservations." He offered his hand, and this time his grip was firm. "It'll be our privilege to have you with us again. Have you thought where you'd like to go? With your seniority, you can pick and choose. Here, let me show you what **we** have."

As Morgan studied the screen, the years rolled back. Jaspre, she noticed at once, was listed. **To** finally see those colored snows . . .

About the Author

Mary Caraker was born and grew up in northwestern Oregon, but in recent years has made her home in San Francisco. She attended Willamette University, the University of Oregon, and San Francisco State University. She has a B.A. and an M.A. in English Literature, and has taught English in public and private schools. She is currently working as a free-lance writer and has published a number of short stories. SEVEN WORLDS is her first novel.